THE
CONFESSION
CLUB

THE CONFESSION CLUB

A Novel

Elizabeth Berg

BALLANTINE BOOKS

NEW YORK

2020 Ballantine Books Trade Paperback Edition

Copyright © 2019 by Elizabeth Berg
Book club guide copyright © 2020 by Penguin Random House LLC

Published in the United States by Ballantine Books, an imprint of Random House, a division of Penguin Random House LLC, New York.

BALLANTINE and the HOUSE colophon are registered trademarks of Penguin Random House LLC.
RANDOM HOUSE BOOK CLUB and colophon are trademarks of Penguin Random House LLC.

Originally published in hardcover in the United States by Random House, an imprint and division of Penguin Random House LLC, in 2019.

Grateful acknowledgment is made to Warren Nelson for permission to reprint an excerpt from "Down at Patsy's Bar," copyright © 2003 by Warren Nelson. Reprinted by permission of the author.

LIBRARY OF CONGRESS CATALOGING-IN-PUBLICATION DATA
Names: Berg, Elizabeth, author.
Title: The confession club : a novel / Elizabeth Berg.
Description: First edition. | New York : Random House, [2019]
Identifiers: LCCN 2019007966| ISBN 9781984855190 (paperback) |
ISBN 9781984855183 (ebook)
Classification: LCC PS3552.E6996 C66 2019 | DDC 813/.54—dc23
LC record available at https://lccn.loc.gov/2019007966

Printed in the United States of America on acid-free paper

randomhousebooks.com
randomhousebookclub.com

2 4 6 8 9 7 5 3 1

Title-page images: © iStockphoto.com

Book design by Dana Leigh Blanchette

For Phyllis Florin
and
Marianne Quasha

The mystical teachings
do not erase sorrow.
They say, here is your life.
What will you do with it?

—Yehoshua November,
from *Two Worlds Exist*

THE
CONFESSION
CLUB

Spill It, Girls

❧

For Confession Club, Joanie Benson is going to make Black Cake. It seems right: dense, mysterious, full of odd little bits and pieces of surprising ingredients. It was seeing *The Belle of Amherst* that gave her the idea. Joanie had enjoyed the play, not so much for all that "Truth must dazzle gradually" stuff—although, come to think of it, didn't that fit right in with Confession Club? But no, never mind Emily Dickinson drifting around the stage in her white dress, tossing off lines of poetry that made others in the audience quietly gasp; Joanie was fixated on the cake Emily was making. Emily gave out the recipe in a rush of ingredients, but of course one is not prepared to copy down a recipe in a darkened theater, and besides, Joanie wasn't persuaded that it was a real recipe, anyway. But in the lobby afterward, the theater did a very nice thing: they served Black Cake, and Joanie had some, and it was delicious.

When she was driving home from the play with her friend Gretchen Buckwalter, Joanie waited to get off the freeway to talk. No matter who is driving, they don't talk on the freeway, they don't even listen to the radio. (Joanie is a better driver than Gretchen in the sense that she still will make left turns. Gretchen goes around the block, so that she can make a right.) But once they were on the two-lane highway leading to Mason, driving past open fields, Joanie relaxed her grip on the wheel. She told Gretchen she was going to find the recipe for Black Cake and make it for Confession Club, which, don't forget, was at her house this Wednesday.

"What?" asked Gretchen. She hadn't been listening; she'd been trying to catch a glimpse of herself in the side-view mirror, never mind the lack of light. Gretchen is sixty-nine years old and one of those former knockouts who just can't stop mourning the loss of her looks. She admits that if she didn't think God would punish her by making her die on the OR table—and if she could afford it—she'd have every bit of plastic surgery she could, head to toe. Gretchen knows she is shallow in this regard, but she kind of enjoys being shallow this way. And anyway, she believes her fixation with looking good helps make her store, Size Me Up!, the success that it is. Her boutique is for women of a certain age who still want to fight the good fight, as Gretchen sees it. She has lots of cape-y and drape-y things that cover a multitude of sins. She also sells a lot of jewel-toned scarves that seem to say, *Yoo hoo! Up here! Look up* here!

Her dressing rooms have curtains that close all the way and her sales staff is trained never to open those curtains—if another size is needed, the customer's arm comes out when she is good and ready to snatch the hanger. The lighting in the dressing rooms is adequate but merciful, due to the use of pink bulbs; the carpeting is thick, and the white leather benches for sitting on are not those tiny insubstantial things you see in other dressing rooms. Best of all, good music is always playing and wine is available, too, should you need it to counteract the shock of seeing yourself in a full-length mirror in your underwear.

Joanie, on the other hand, has always been satisfied with her admittedly plain-Jane looks. Who cares? She looks friendly! She *is* friendly! She still wears the bob she wore in high school and she eschews any makeup beyond mascara and pink lipstick. She has a wide-eyed expression that seems to say, *Well,* hi *there!* She doesn't mind the extra weight she carries. She thinks Gretchen is a little nuts for the way she is always dieting, for the way she holds on to her long red hair and hoop earrings. But Gretchen does have her good qualities. And for heaven's sake, they've been friends since they were both in their high school's production of *South Pacific.* Gretchen, a senior, was Nellie, the lead; Joanie, a freshman, was one of the native girls wearing a "grass" skirt made of newspaper strips painted green, and a bikini top. She used to help Gretchen run lines and they just hit it off, despite the age difference that then seemed immense and now seems negligible.

"What did you say?" Gretchen asked Joanie, and Joanie told her again that she was going to make the Black Cake Emily Dickinson had talked about. She said she'd go to the library where she used to work and research the recipe. Joanie liked any excuse to go to the library; she liked it especially if a patron came up and said they missed her.

"That was your takeaway from the performance?" Gretchen asked. "The cake?"

During the play, Gretchen herself was all Miss Pittypat, her bosom practically heaving, her eyes damp enough to require Gretchen dabbing at them now and then with a balled-up Kleenex. Gretchen was the first to rise for the standing ovation, which the actress did deserve — my goodness, all those lines, all that *feeling* — but Joanie got a little annoyed that she had to move her jacket and purse and then push up hard on the armrests to stand, which hurt her elbows, because even though she's only sixty-five, she has awful arthritis. Then she had to endure what she thought was excessive — really, just excessive — applause from the crowd (one person shouting, "*Brava!*" with a rolled *r*, for heaven's sake!). All that clapping and clapping and clapping, Joanie's hands got tired, but who wanted to be the party pooper and stop clapping first?

Well, that's what you get when you leave the sensible

little town of Mason, Missouri, and drive all the way to Columbia, everyone putting on airs all over the place, even the waitstaff in the restaurants: "Good evening, I'm Thaddeus, I'll be your server for the evening. May I start you out with one of our signature cocktails?" And then that business of not writing down anything she orders, which always makes Joanie a nervous wreck. Joanie prefers the greeting offered by the waitstaff in restaurants she frequents in Mason: "Well, look who's here. The usual, hon?"

Still, one must endeavor to incorporate a little culture into one's life. One can't rely on the Town Players and the Gazebo Summertime Band and Poulet Frisée Olé for everything. Joanie also attends the monthly poetry readings at the library, but that is less culture than charity, Grace Haddock and her impenetrable lines of alliteration every time. *Alliteration does not a poem make,* thinks Joanie, and she's not the only one, judging by the gritted teeth and crossed arms of the people around her whenever Grace grips the edges of the podium and lets fly. Most of the poems the participants present aren't very good. Still, each time Joanie walks home from one of those readings, she thinks about something she heard. Once a man wrote about his first kiss. "Lips as soft as petals," he'd said shyly, his head down, and it made Joanie go all melty inside, which only went to prove that she was, too, a romantic person, never mind what others sometimes said about her. (Once, at Confession Club, they were talking about first

loves and someone said Joanie's first—and only—love was
Dewey Decimal.)

The poet that night said something else, too, about eyes
shining in the dark, and Joanie liked thinking about that,
those young eyes, that first kiss. It made her think about
her own first kiss, which was in a basement and, oh, Lord,
it was her cousin, which she will never tell anyone, and
she hopes he never will, either. He doesn't live in Mason
anymore, thank goodness. It still makes her squinch up
inside to think about that kiss, which was the best kiss she
ever had, and isn't that sad, to have had your best kiss
when you were twelve years old? If she'd known that at the
time, she might have felt like throwing in the towel. But
there's more to life than sex, especially at her age. She's at
a kind of tipping point, she feels. Not young anymore, not
old, but looking down at old like it's a pool she's going to
have to dive into soon. But not yet. Not yet. She's glad
many of her friends are younger. She and Gretchen agree
that it's good to be around younger people. Things rub off.
Totally, Joanie has begun saying, with no self-consciousness
at all. Gretchen has yet to follow, but she does say *cool*.
She also says that *cool* was created more by their genera-
tion than by this one. So.

Confession Club started accidentally. It used to be Third
Sunday Supper Club, formed from a group of eight
women ranging in age from their thirties to their seventies,

all of whom had taken baking classes with Iris Winters. After the women grew comfortable enough with one another, they began sharing things they'd done wrong. It just became, as they say, a *thing*, and after a while, they decided to meet more often, twice a month, then weekly. At each meeting, someone confessed to something she'd done recently or long ago. And just like in church, it made people feel better, because at the end of the meeting the group said in unison to the confessor, "Go in peace." Very powerful words, whatever your belief system. On certain days, those words could make you feel like crying.

One time Leah Short, their senior member at seventy-seven, had too many margaritas with dinner (Gretchen had made empanadas and enchiladas and even flan), and Leah said sloppily, waving her hand for emphasis, "Go in peach." And then the next week someone brought a peach-colored scarf, and now it's a tradition: whoever is forgiven wears the peach scarf home. And then that person brings it back the next week all hand-washed and ironed and ready for the next sinner.

Naturally, it was endlessly fascinating, what people confessed to. There was a saying someone shared at an early meeting: *The truth is always interesting.* So, too, an honest confession. And it wasn't necessarily the sin that was interesting; it was the willingness to say, *There. Have a good look at my imperfections.* It made you feel better about your own.

There weren't many times when people missed Confession Club. Joanie feels it's her job to keep people on track, though. If it was your turn to confess, why, you had to come and confess something.

Rosemary Dolman once confessed to taking cookies off a grocery store shelf at Betterman's, sampling them, disliking them, and then putting them back on the shelf.

All the women laughed when Rosemary shared this, and she said, "Well, I am very surprised by this reaction. I am *upset* about this, and I haven't told anyone, and I thought surely I could confess it here and get some sympathy and some advice! I feel like this was effectively stealing. More than that, it sounds like it was done by someone a little . . . out of it. I fear I'm getting old and strange like my Aunt Pookie, who makes no sense whatsoever anymore, but holds forth at family dinners like she's royalty. All people do around her is hold their mouths real tight together so they won't burst out laughing."

"How old are you again?" Dodie Hicks asked. Dodie is north of seventy, though she won't say how far north. "I'm Minneapolis, not International Falls, okay?" she says. "When I hit the big 8-0 we'll have a party with dancing boys."

Dodie still dyes her hair a severe black. It makes her face look alarmingly white. And then she draws on long, coal-black eyebrows and wears black mascara and blue eye shadow and blush that Gretchen says makes her look slapped. In the spirit of honesty between friends, Gretchen told Dodie that, and Dodie, in the same spirit, told her to mind her own business. Dodie still smokes, too, though she is courteous enough to smoke outside, even on the coldest winter days. But her cigarettes are unfiltered, so she is always doing that nasty thing of picking tobacco off her tongue and going, *Ptuh! Ptuh!*

On that day when Rosemary confessed her fear of becoming odd and Dodie asked Rosemary how old she was, Rosemary took a while to answer. She is one of those women with elegant bone structure who creams her face religiously with ridiculously expensive placenta-y things and wears a lot of nice jewelry given to her by her husband, who owns Mason's only car dealership, Dolman Chevrolet (his sign says, IF YOU DON'T WANT A CHEVY, YOU DON'T NEED A CAR), and she will probably always look at least a little glamorous, even in her coffin. But when she was asked her age, she looked over at Dodie, her chin lifted high, and said, "I'm turning sixty."

"When?" Dodie asked. The women liked when there were birthdays. Cake.

"In a year and a half."

A moment of confusion, and then Dodie said, "Well, then you're turning fifty-nine, aren't you?"

"I'm just going to get it over with," Rosemary said. "I'm just going to say I'm turning sixty."

"The point is," said Anne McCrae, who had recently turned seventy-four, and had brought the most darling cake to the group for her party—it had been made to look like her poodle—"putting those cookies back on the shelf?

That's nothing. In fact, I think that store sort of deserves it. They're snobby. The displays are so fancy you don't feel you can touch them. You stand in front of the cheeses and it's like they're whispering to one another about you, in French. And whenever they give out samples in that store, they cut the tiniest little pieces and then watch like a hawk that you don't take two. And everything is so expensive!"

"That's true," said Rosemary. "And I guess that was part of it—those cookies cost twelve dollars. Twelve dollars! I thought for that price they'd be delicious, and they were from Europe and everything, so I threw them in the cart. I was hungry, so I had one, and they were *awful*. I didn't want to pay twelve dollars for cookies I'd just throw away, so I put them back on the shelf. And then I was so ashamed, I ran out of the store and just left my full basket there. Which I guess was also a sin."

"That's nothing, either," said Anne. "People do that all the time. I guess there are emergencies or something."

"There were *chicken* breasts in there!" Rosemary said.

"I'm sure the store has insurance for that kind of thing."

"And as for it being odd behavior," said Leah, "you don't know the half of it. When you get older, you *do* start acting old and funny. And wearing Poise pads."

Rosemary's mouth hung open. If a woman could still look attractive with her mouth hanging open, Rosemary did. Then, "Oh, my God," she said softly. And with tears trembling in her eyes, she said, "I don't think I want to live anymore. If this is what's going to start happening, maybe I've had enough."

There followed such a ruckus, such a loud consensus of outraged disapproval, that Rosemary folded her arms over herself, ashamed, and said no more.

"You know, Rosemary, that wasn't really much of a confession," said Toots Monroe.

Toots is stout and practical, a devotee of pastel-colored pants suits and jewel-eyed animal pins, and she's ever cheerful. She's forty-seven and looks a good five years younger—great skin, great blond hair that she wears in a long bob with side bangs. She is the newly elected president of the town council, and has about her an air of can-do. It's comforting. It's like being around a man who knows how to fix everything, only you don't have to put up with a man. (Toots's own often-voiced position on men is that they should be kept in closets and taken out only when needed, like a vacuum cleaner.) She is sometimes a little tone-deaf, but there is no one who doesn't like Toots. She'd never do anything to hurt anyone on purpose, and if you need anything, she's the one to ask.

Toots told Rosemary, "A confession is when you talk about something you did wrong. Refusing to pay for something that didn't taste good—well, putting the cookies back on the shelf—was not really a sin, it was just tacky."

Rosemary reached under her chair for her purse. "I have to go."

"No you don't," Joanie said. "You're just mad. And embarrassed. Let's talk this through." And so they did. And then Leah offered a bona-fide confession, which was that she used to steal money from the collection basket. She would pretend she was putting something in, but she was taking something out.

"That's pretty bad," said Karen Lungren, who was, after all, married to the minister over at Good Shepherd. But when Karen asked what kind of church and Leah said, "Catholic," Karen said, "Oh, well, that's okay then."

Karen is the youngest member of Confession Club, at thirty-five. She is an athletic and highly disciplined woman who is for the most part rather quiet and circumspect. She's seemingly proper as can be, one of those to always fold her napkin into an exact square after she has finished using it. You feel she makes her bed right after she gets out of it. But every now and then she lets slip the f-bomb and then she apologizes profusely. And the group always forgives her, though they do always make her put a dollar in the Whoops! jar. (Whenever they get to twenty dollars, they give the money to the library to buy new books.)

On the day of Rosemary's confession, just as the women were getting ready to leave, Karen said, "You know, I've been thinking. I move that we open our confessions to things we're generally ashamed of. Like, not necessarily a sin per se, but something that gets in there and just really bothers you."

"Well, exactly," said Rosemary.

"All right," said Toots. "There is a motion on the floor to open up confession to plain shame. Do I have a second?"

"I second the motion," said Anne, wearily.

"All for?" Toots asked. All the women raised their hands.

"Opposed?" Toots asked, and Joanie said, "Toots. We all raised our hands!"

"The motion has passed, and we are adjourned," Toots said, and banged her spoon like a gavel.

Oh, they knew they were mostly silly. They enjoyed being silly, because sometimes you just needed to take a load off. For Pete's sake. You just needed a little levity, and you needed to be on the right side of the yellow light shining out from the dining room window, you needed to be in that pocket of place where you were unequivocally welcome and could at any time slip right out of your shoes.

In the Nighttime

❦

Like most people, Iris Winters has nights when she can't
sleep. It doesn't happen very often, but when it does, Iris
knows better than to fight against it. She might be a little
girl again, her mother standing at the bottom of the stairs
and yelling up for Iris to get out of bed for school. No
fighting against that, either, no matter what the reason.
Iris's mother was a no-nonsense blue-blood Brahmin
whose advice on everything from a headache to heartache
was always the same: *Oh, you'll be all right.*

Usually, Iris's treatment for insomnia is simple enough:
a cup of tea drunk at the kitchen table and a glancing
around at the way things get transformed in the moon-
light; the curtains seem made of fairy cloth. Other times,
she reads or does a little cleaning, tossing out things like
the absurdly tiny safety pins used for attaching price tags
that Iris's daytime mind tells her will come in handy for
*some*thing. (You can take the thrifty New Englander out of
New England . . .)

Tonight, though, Iris sits in a bedroom chair with Homer, her cat, in her lap, looking at the empty street below, mindlessly twisting a strand of hair. She is plagued with ill-formed questions about where she is and why, with worries about how she will end up. Things about which she is unalterably sure in the daytime become slippery on nights like this; even the simple joy of teaching her baking classes in Mason, this tiny town she now calls home, disappears, and a cynical voice at the back of her brain snickers at the very idea. It is as though a lynchpin that holds her to her place on earth has been snatched away, and she is free-floating and full of doubt. In addition to that, a kind of longing she has experienced all her life bears down upon her. It is a longing not for something she can name, but for something she cannot.

So what does Iris do? She grabs her notebook and plans another class. When Chocolate Met Peanut Butter. Suddenly, thunder rumbles, and rain begins drumming on the roof. She stops writing to look up. It is a primal response, Iris thinks, something humans will never lose, the way we look up when the rain comes. We've seen it before, but every time is different. It is as though we ask ourselves, *What will happen this time?*

Man on the Run

❦

In the old place, John knew all the routines. That's because in Chicago, John created all the routines. Late-morning breakfasts at the McDonald's on State Street, where they'd let you be, an upstairs table by the window that the six of them squeezed around: Proud Mary, because she was proud of nothing; Fred Astaire, who couldn't walk without tripping; Hairy, who was bald; Genius, who wasn't one; Stretch, who was four feet eleven; and John, who would not tolerate nicknames, having endured quite enough of them growing up. When someone suggested he could at least use "Sarge" as a nickname to honor his service in Vietnam, John offered only a look.

But yes, breakfast at Mickey D's, sharing an assortment of whatever their pooled resources could get them. Then off to the library, where they could spread out. You could read the paper or magazines or books or screw around on the Internet. You could attend a lecture—on a dare, John had once attended one on opera, but you know what? It was kind of great. The guy giving the lecture had hands that shook. John could relate to him. The songs he played for them—arias—were so beautiful they twisted you up a bit. You could also take a free class, though only Hairy ever did that—one Christmas he made a gingerbread house that he shared with the rest of them after he'd eaten the roof and most of the gumdrops, in private.

For people without a home, the library was Mercy Land. You could warm up or cool off. You could sit in a comfortable chair. You could clean up a bit, though you had to be careful about that. They didn't like homeless people cleaning up in the bathroom. They didn't like homeless people wrapped in layers of clothes like mummies, with boots made from garbage bags and duct tape; it scared the little kids. They also didn't like homeless people who smelled, and if you smelled bad enough you would be quietly asked to leave. They'd give you a list of places where you could shower, but what they maybe didn't know is if you showered in such places, good luck.

John grew up with a mother who insisted on his looking neat as a pin. They weren't rich, not by a long shot; they weren't even comfortable. But his mother made sure he was clean and his clothes were pressed, and she kept him healthy, too. He saw a doctor for regular checkups and for any illness, even if his parents didn't. He went to the dentist twice a year—one Dr. Cornelius Standard, a man who helped maintain his business by handing out lollipops to kids at the end of every visit. And for all the complaints you could make about the U.S. Army, John did get good healthcare there. So when his life fell apart and he ended up on the street more often than not, he still kept clean. Oftentimes, he looked better than people he knew who did have homes. He would spend money on a laundromat, and he'd sweep up in a barbershop in exchange for a haircut and a shave. He took advantage of dental schools offering free services—free but for the gratitude you were expected to offer—and the results were nearly always pretty good. As for bathing, he had secrets he didn't share with the others, who would have ruined things for him. For example, some hotels had swimming pools that could serve as a bathtub—early afternoons, those pools were almost always empty. You walked into those hotels like you knew what you were doing—that was key. Like you knew what you were doing and you were in a hurry and a bit perturbed, like everyone else. Sometimes you could steal things off a maid's cart, but that was advanced.

Occasionally—often, even—a woman would take him home to her apartment and he'd shower there. "You get by on your looks, don't you?" one woman asked him. She was a social worker, a nice person. He allowed as how he did get by that way. Sometimes.

You weren't supposed to sleep in the library, although many people did sleep there. If you slept too long or snored too loudly, or if you slept in a bathroom stall, you got kicked out. In the summer, it was no big deal: go out and find a place in a park. In winter, you tried hard to stay awake: Take little walks. Chat up a sympathetic librarian (though you had to be careful to notice when they'd had enough, when they leaned back, or shifted their gaze to over your shoulder, or said, "Okay, then, so . . ."). You could sit in a group with other homeless people and have a conversation, although most times those "conversations" were just bitching sessions about the red tape involved in getting anything you were entitled to from the government.

When the library closed, there were some bars they could go to. Proud Mary always went in first: she was a remarkably pretty woman who also believed in keeping clean, so she parted the seas. The rest of them followed like connected cars on a train. Some of the bars they went to had free food: hardboiled eggs; cheese and crackers. If you didn't take too much, you could have some with a beer that you could nurse for a good half hour.

Now and then, John donned his custodian's uniform, a brown cotton jumpsuit with MANNY embroidered on it that he found in someone's trash. Before security tightened, he wore it into schools when they were having PTO meetings, and he would help clean up afterward—miraculously, no one the wiser. Only once, someone who was also cleaning said, "You new here?" and John nodded. That was the end of it. There were always cookies left over at PTO meetings, which he was always offered, and if the coffee they served was in one of those handy cardboard containers, he was allowed that, too.

Sometimes he would go to funeral lunches held in the basement of churches, though in those instances he wore a dark, somber suit he bought for six dollars at Goodwill—an investment that paid off. A lot of good food was served after a funeral, much of it even homemade—the deceased's favorite foods and whatnot. But sometimes grief made people eat a lot, grief and the realization that life really did come to an end. They'd go back to the food table again and again: *I'm alive!* But at one funeral, no one seemed much in the mood to eat, and he'd brought the group tin pans of salad and macaroni and cheese and lasagna, trays of roast beef and turkey sandwiches, all kinds of cupcakes, even plastic cutlery. ("You want to take this home?" the women who were dishing the stuff out told him. "Makes for an easier cleanup for us!" And then when John thanked them, they said, "Sure, sorry for your loss.")

It was hard to keep the food looking nice when it was shoved quickly into plastic bags, as he did that day, but most of the group didn't mind. Everyone was long past being picky about such things, except for Genius. He was like a toddler, didn't like different kinds of foods touching. And once, when someone offered to buy him lunch at a sandwich place, he said he was hoping for tacos from down the street. He got them, too; that was an earth angel he ran into that day. Most people you hit up for money to buy a meal ignored you. Sometimes when you said, "Spare change?" they'd say, "No thanks," and smirk, and elbow the person they were walking with.

It was usually midday when his group asked for money—nights were too crowded and funky. Genius and Stretch liked to stand on the ramps leading to and from the highway. People seemed to feel scared for you there, and were more likely to call you over and give you something. They told John that one guy who had staked out a place on the ramp brought his dog along, a little beagle mix, and he'd sit the dog on the concrete median, where he effectively begged for the man because the dog was so cute. Lots of people gave that guy money. Maybe they should get a dog, John's group said, and John said no.

They ate at Taco Bell. Subway. The Portillo's on Clark Street. Certain diners had cheap soup and you could ask for extra crackers. People coming from restaurants might give you their doggie bags. And sometimes a do-gooder would take you into a restaurant they were going into and buy you a meal and then sit with you while you ate. The danger there was they could pepper you with questions, try to get you to go to this social-service place or that, try to find out exactly why you weren't working, just generally be in your business. Occasionally they wanted to buy drugs and figured you'd know how and where. And that maybe, given that you'd just eaten courtesy of them, you'd buy the drugs for them. One time, some guy who said he was a famous writer took Proud Mary to a fancy restaurant on Michigan Avenue after he bought her an entire outfit—a red top, white pants, sandals, a purse, even silver hoop earrings and a bracelet—at Nordstrom's. He'd made her miserable with his oozing empathy and penetrating gaze. Halfway through the meal, she excused herself to go to the ladies' room, changed back into the street clothes she'd stuffed into her bag, and cut out. She left all the things the guy had bought her in the bathroom. Everyone approved but Hairy, who wouldn't let up on her and kept saying, "You prolly could have *sold* them things back to Nordstrom's, Mary!"

All in all, it wasn't worth it to accept gifts that were too big. Eat with your friends or alone. Or don't eat. They all got used to that. One day, bonanza; the next day your gut ached from hunger. "Can your stomach try to eat itself?" Genius asked once. It didn't seem like an entirely unreasonable question.

Now John is in a new place. He got restless and hit the road. He left without saying a word and hitched as far as this little town called Mason, in Missouri, where he saw an abandoned farmhouse from the road. He asked the trucker to let him off, and he's been staying here for a week now. Best place he's ever found. The house is far off the road and mostly obscured by overgrown lilac bushes in full bloom. Birds are everywhere, singing their hearts out every morning, including a bachelor mockingbird, who courts the ladies with his playlist of imitative calls.

Best of all, John can bathe in the creek that runs behind the house. Oh, it's cold when you sit in it, but you are out soon enough, and he has a blanket he can wrap up in to dry off. He washes his clothes in the creek after he washes himself, and lays his wrung-out shirts and dungarees on the fence to dry in the fresh air and sunshine. Deluxe.

Last evening, just before the sun went down, John lay in the grass and watched a gaggle of geese in a wobbly chevron honking their way across a blood-red sky, clouds like puffs of smoke, and it was the prettiest thing he'd seen since his group in Chicago went to the Art Institute on free day and John settled in before Monet's haystacks.

Behind the house is a barn where the sweet-sour scent of livestock still lingers, and behind that, fenced-in fields where wildflowers have taken over: beardtongue, tickseed, prairie clover, button snakeroot. It's good to see untended things thriving.

When John was in his old life and married for the little while he was, he and his wife would talk sometimes about what was happening to the environment. Laura was such a sensitive soul; she would weep in despair, and John would shrug and tell her everything would be fine. Not for people, but for the earth. It would all come back. They wouldn't be here, but the earth would come back, green shoots curling out of ruin, nature insisting upon itself. He found that comforting. She did not.

He thinks about her less than he used to, but he still thinks about her a lot. When it snows, he thinks of how she liked the snow. When he sees baskets of apples at farmers' markets, he thinks of her pies. When he sees a woman whose hair is that shiny brown, when he sees a woman singing to herself, when he sees striped socks or a woman deeply engrossed in a book or bent to speak to a child, he thinks of her. He tries to forget why she left him, but of course he will never forget that. Or forgive himself for it.

He came to Mason with some money; he's got just under a hundred bucks from a run of good days he had back in Chicago. A couple of days into his stay here, he walked into town and bought some tools and a can opener at Smith's Hardware, and he bought some seeds and to-mato starter plants, too. He had to—those seed packets with their beautiful images of food, the tomato plants nearly straining to bust out of their tiny containers, and him being on a farm with all that land.

They were nice people at the hardware store, as relaxed and easy as their name. After he was done there, he went to the barbershop, then ate breakfast at Polly's Henhouse. They gave him the eye a little at Polly's, but he sat respect-fully at the counter for his English muffin and black cof-fee. He didn't pocket any jam or butter, though he had planned to. But some black-haired waitress named Mon-ica seemed to have eyes in the back of her head. Nice enough, real nice, in fact, but eyes in the back of her head, one of those don't-piss-me-off types. The prices were rea-sonable, and the food was good. He'd mind his manners so he could come back. Salisbury steak was on the menu. Thanksgiving sandwiches. Chicken croquettes in yellow gravy.

He planted behind the barn, never mind that it was

only the third week of May. Imagine. Tomatoes. Basil. Carrots. Butter lettuce and romaine. Sweet peas. Cukes. For free, more or less. He swept out the house with a broom he found in someone's trash, cleaned the windows with newspapers and a half-full bottle of Windex he found there, too, brought home a busted-up bicycle he might be able to fix. When his phone rings with a call from Proud Mary, who was nominally his girlfriend, he doesn't answer. When it rings with a call from anyone else he used to hang around with, he doesn't answer, either. Lift the page on the Magic Slate, man. Got to.

It's warm today, and after John checks on the garden, he sits down, leans against the barn wall, and settles in for some thinking time. This is the most peaceful place he's ever been, and maybe the most beautiful. At night, in the absence of city light, he sees so many stars that the dark sky looks salted. Laura wanted to live out in the country, and what did he say? No. But maybe she was right. Maybe it would have saved them.

He is relieved to know that he can still use a library for so many things. It's a little library, of course, but they have plugs for charging his phone, they have a couple of computers for public use. He hasn't seen any other people he thinks are homeless, but then he doesn't look particularly homeless, either. In the farmhouse, he found a stash of men's clothes in a plastic bag on the floor of a closet. There were also shoes that fit him well enough: sneakers, some black dress shoes, and a pair of barn boots. He washed the clothes at Lila's Laundromat (WHERE KLEAN IS KING!), and, voilà, he could practically run for office now. He found some chipped dishes in the kitchen cupboards, he found tarnished silverware in a stuck drawer he pried open, and there were a few pots and pans way back in one of the lower cupboards. He found a girlie calendar from 1959, and a stack of record albums, mostly jazz, which surprised him. He found a metal bed frame in the rafters of the barn and brought it into the living room. He stuffed some shirts with hay for a mattress. His backpack is his pillow. There's an armchair in the basement he might bring up if there aren't too many mice in it. The kitchen table he did bring up from the basement. It's one of those old 1950s Formica ones, a turquoise color, and there are four turquoise-and-white vinyl chairs, rips in every one of them, but they are sturdy enough for sitting. He ferries back and forth plastic water containers—he bought a couple of containers new and now refills them in the bathrooms of gas stations. Next time he goes to town, maybe he'll find some cheap towels. He knows that Our Lady of Peace has a thrift store but it's only open on Thursdays—hard for him to remember when it's Thursday. Without a job, he finds that his life lacks the kind of structure that makes specific days matter.

He builds a little fire outside when he needs heat; the nightly breeze is his air conditioner, the woods his bathroom. What else does a man need?

A yellow butterfly lands on John's knee and he sud-

denly crashes. Under the blue sky and in view of the milk-
weed, he sobs. Because . . . oh, you know. The warmth of
the day, the sun like a blanket across his shoulders. The
near-lyrical pattern of the butterfly's flight away from him.
Himself alive, and that a sin when he watched so many
others fall. Himself still upon the earth: a man with fingers, feeling fingerless.

But. He gets up. He'll see what he can afford at the
hardware store to maybe fix the bicycle. He'll see if the
bakery has thrown out yesterday's day-old. He'll find out
where the dump is; always good stuff at a dump. Begging
on the streets won't work here; soon, he'll need to find day
jobs. It scares him, but he'll do it so he can stay here. For
now.

A Favor

✦

Wednesday morning, on what she thought would be a day off, Iris Winters rings Joanie Benson's doorbell three times before Joanie yanks it open. She's wearing a white bathrobe and has a towel wrapped lopsidedly around her head.

"I'm so sorry," Joanie says breathlessly. "I'm running late. I was in the shower, and I took way longer than I meant to. I always do that. I go into the shower wanting to be an environmentalist and come out a hedonist." She steps aside. "Come in, come in, I'm so grateful you were able to come. You're the *real* cake doctor!"

Iris waves her hand. "Don't give me too much credit. I've never made Black Cake." She does not add that she's never heard of it.

Joanie leads her into the kitchen. Ingredients and bowls are all over the place. There's a cutting board with a knife lying on it that has yet to be used, from the looks of it.

"I have to have this cake done by five, and I also have to make dinner for six. I don't know what I was thinking. I printed out the recipe without really looking at it, thinking, you know, 'Oh, it's just a cake, how hard can it be?' But then this morning, I read it all the way through, and, Lord!"

"May I see the recipe?" Iris asks. Joanie hands her the printout and Iris surveys the long list of ingredients: ten eggs; a pound each of prunes, raisins, dates, currants, cherries; candied citrus peel; cherry brandy; Angostura bitters . . . The time to make it is five hours, and it's now eleven-fifteen. She looks up at Joanie. "First of all, do you even have all this stuff?"

"Well, of course I don't have all that stuff! I was going to get up this morning, go to the store, get what I needed for the cake and the dinner. But then when I read the list of ingredients, I just . . . well, I panicked and called you."

Iris scans the directions. Grind macerated fruit to a coarse paste; caramelize sugar until it's almost black, add boiling water (furious steam here); it may stiffen up when you try to add it to the batter. . . .

"This is pretty advanced," she tells Joanie.

"Right?" Joanie clutches her bathrobe under her chin.

"How about if I help you make another kind of cake?"

"Oh, no. I can't do that."

"Why not?"

"Because I told everyone I was making Black Cake."

"I see." One thing Iris likes about living here is the way you can pretty much count on everyone keeping their word. There are times she misses Boston, where she moved from, but more and more, she's happy to call this place home.

"Why don't we see if there's another recipe for Black Cake that might be a bit simpler?" she asks Joanie.

"Oh, I didn't even think of that!" Joanie says. "I was just so happy to see a recipe for it at all that I printed it out right away. They were making it in the 1800s—can you imagine? Probably before. And they didn't even have microwaves!"

"Where's your computer?" Iris asks, and Joanie takes her to a little desk in the living room. Iris googles "Black Cake" and finds a much more user-friendly recipe. "This is the one," she says, "but we'll still need to get going—it takes several hours. And we'll have to make browning for this one. Hmm. I've been meaning to try that—it's basically just burnt sugar and water."

Joanie sits down on the sofa and sighs. "I don't know, maybe this *is* too hard. I'm going to have to serve something else. I'm so disappointed."

"We can do it," Iris says. "Why don't you start on dinner? Don't worry about the cake for now. I'll go to the grocery store and then to the liquor store—the one on the county line is huge. I forgot the name of it, but it should have port wine and white rum."

"County Line Liquors?"

"Oh. Right."

"I never go there. It's way too far."

It's a ten-minute car ride, at the most. Iris says, "It's no problem. I'll head out now. When I come back, we'll make the cake together. It'll go much more quickly with two of us."

"Let me give you some money."

"Pay me later. Just put a check mark by all the things on the recipe that you need."

After Joanie checks off the items she needs and thanks Iris again (and again), Iris gets in her car and heads for the grocery store. Miraculously, she finds everything she needs, though the brandied cherries and candied orange peel are retrieved from some apparently little-used storage space in the back, and have the dust to prove it. "Still good, though!" the man who got them for her proclaims, pointing to the expiration dates. "Makin' a fruitcake?" he asks.

"Something like that," Iris says.

"I hate fruitcake!" he says cheerfully, and Iris says, "I do, too."

"Why you makin' it then?" he asks, and Iris says, "Long story."

"I bet you got some old aunt or somethin'," the man says, and so Iris feels obliged to hurriedly fill him in.

Finally, she's on the old two-lane blacktop that still has telephone wires running along either side of it. What is romantic about telephone poles? Nothing, Iris supposes, and yet she finds them romantic. Birds on the wires lined up like notes on a staff. Many of the poles listing slightly to the right or the left. You might even see a heart carved into one here and there, initials inside it. What tender hope is in carved initials, affection made public that old-fashioned way.

She turns off the radio and lowers her car window all the way. Spring and fall are her favorite seasons, with spring having a slight edge: the robins, the reemergence of life that was buried under snow. There are banks of lilacs blooming in front of many houses, especially as she gets farther out into the country, and when she drives by them, she slows down. Iris likes the scent of lilacs as much as anyone, but she also likes their beautiful colors: white, light violet, dark violet, pink. In her bedroom, she has a small oil painting of deep-purple lilacs that she bought at a Newbury Street art gallery, and it's her favorite painting. She's just thinking you don't see that dark shade often enough when she spies an overgrown stand of them in front of a farmhouse. The house is clearly abandoned. What would be the harm? On the way back from the liquor store, she'll take a bunch of them.

It takes longer than Iris anticipated at the liquor store, because the cashier—FRITZ, his name tag says—and the customer ahead of her are showing each other pictures of their grandchildren on their phones. "This one here is potty-trained already," says the customer.

Next the customer wonders aloud whether he should buy some beef jerky. "It ain't gonna go *bad*, Fred," says the cashier. "And take it from me. A day will come when you'll be setting at a train crossing, one of those long freight trains going through, and you'll be wishing you had something to chew on, and there it will be in your glove compartment. Wa-la."

"Oh, all right," Fred says. "I'll get some." He takes his time sorting through the various flavors and peering through the bottom portion of his bifocals to read the ingredients. Despite her time crunch, Iris doesn't get irritated. To her, the man is fascinating to watch. He's about eighty, she supposes, dressed in clean bib jeans and a white T-shirt, with a red flannel shirt serving as a kind of jacket. He's got wire-rimmed glasses and a comfortable paunch, thick white hair and beard. He looks like an off-season Santa Claus. And Fritz the clerk is an interesting counterpoint: in his forties, Iris would guess, a thin and wiry frame, a nervous talker, a wildly prominent Adam's apple, a few strands of light-brown hair raked over his head. He wears a dark-green apron over a white shirt and black pants; a wristwatch is loose on his arm. She stands waiting. And waiting. She doesn't pull out her phone to pass the time because she might miss something.

Iris has changed since she moved to Mason. In keeping with the pace of life here, she's slowed down in everything but her morning walks. She's become more tolerant and appreciative of people's eccentricities. It's the way folks are here; there's a willingness to let people be that rubs off.

Jason and Abby Summers, the people who live next door to Iris, own the small but well-curated Menagerie Bookshop. They are relatively new to Mason as well, having moved here a couple of years ago from Chicago, and sometimes Iris goes over for dinner with them and their twelve-year-old son, Link—casual, last-minute affairs, the invitation issued from their front porch to hers. After dinner, when Link has gone off to his room, the adults sometimes talk about whether the charm they've found here can last, whether small towns can continue to retain their character, their kindness and basic sense of decency. They agree that it has something to do with the smallness of the population. It's harder to be horrible to someone you see every day.

It takes a good twenty minutes before Iris is back on the road with the ingredients for the cake—and with her own beef jerky, it might as well be said, teriyaki flavor. When she approaches the lilacs, she checks her watch. It wouldn't take long to get them, but she'd be in a hurry, and she doesn't want to be in a hurry when she gathers lilacs. She might want first to sit under the tree and lean against the trunk and do absolutely nothing. She'll come back. Her class tomorrow (Super-Fast Sticky Buns) isn't until eleven. She'll have plenty of time in the morning; she is now and forever an early riser. All hope is in the early morning, is what Iris thinks.

This time when Joanie answers the door, she's dressed in jeans and a plaid shirt. Beneath a yellow kerchief, her hair is in rollers, and she points to them, saying, "I think I'm the only one in America who still uses these. My grandson calls them 'roller coasters.' How much do I owe you?" After Iris tells her, Joanie goes upstairs and returns with cash. "I keep my money in a pillowcase in my linen closet," she says. "I've had it with banks."

My goodness, Iris thinks, but says nothing. They don't have time to explore the erosion of trust in American institutions; they have a cake to make.

When they go into the kitchen, Iris is glad to see that the cake ingredients Joanie did have are neatly lined up. Iris adds what she bought to the assemblage. "Ready?" she says.

"Ready." Joanie stretches out her hands and cracks her knuckles. "I got everything all done for dinner, so we can just concentrate on the cake. I went and got a premade salad and some nice dinner rolls and I have five-hour stew in the oven. You throw everything together, stick it in the oven, and then nothing to do until you serve it."

Iris turns to face her. "Five-hour stew?"

"It's real good. Everybody who tastes it loves it."

"It cooks for five hours?"

"Yup!"

"At what temperature?"

"Two-fifty. You have to keep it low, of course, when you cook it that long."

Iris sighs. "Do you have a roaster oven?"

Joanie frowns. "No."

"Because the cake has to bake at three-fifty for an hour and a half."

"Well, I thought we could just cook the cake longer."

"If you do that, your crust will be gummy and pale." Iris can practically hear Lucille Howard, the woman who taught her how to bake, saying that, in her pleasantly aggrieved way.

Iris looks at her watch. "What time does your club meet, again?"

"Five o'clock."

"It's a bit after twelve now," Iris says. "The fruit has to soak in the rum for two and a half hours, so—"

"Oh, for God's sake!" Joanie says. "I'm just going to make Rice Krispie Treats! Everybody makes fun of them, but you find me one person who doesn't like them."

"You can still have Black Cake," Iris says calmly. "Pack up the ingredients, and I'll make the cake at my house. I'll deliver it to you. It might not be right at five, but I'll get it here in time for dessert, maybe seven at the latest?"

"Really? My goodness, that would be wonderful! How much?"

"How much what?"

"How much do you charge for that?"

"Oh. Nothing. I'll do it for free."

"Why would you ever do such a thing?" Joanie asks.

Iris shrugs. "You'll take another class from me, won't

you? And tell people about it? And anyway, I kind of love a challenge."

"But this is just above and beyond! How will I ever repay you?"

"Someday, and that day may never come, I will call upon you to do a service for me."

Joanie stares at her. "*The Godfather?*"

"Right. I just watched it again the other night. It still holds up."

"Well," Joanie says, "I know you're kidding, but whatever favor you ask, I will do. That's a promise from the heart. I really, really mean it."

"Could you put all the ingredients in a bag for me?" Iris asks, and Joanie packs them carefully. On her face is that oddly pained expression people sometimes get when they feel guilt mixed with gratitude.

Back home, Iris walks into the kitchen with her heavy bag and drops it on the table. She is just about to start unloading it when she freezes. Upstairs, there is the sound of someone walking around. She swallows, then looks up at the ceiling. "Hello?"

No answer. She moves toward the door, pulling her cellphone from her purse. She is caught between fear for her life and irritation that she can't get going on that cake. But then she hears a familiar voice calling her name.

"Maddy?" There is the sound of someone thumping down the stairs. And then there she is, the beautiful young woman who used to live in this house with Arthur and Lucille, the two old people who took her in as a pregnant teenager. The house is Maddy's—Arthur willed it to her—and she rents it to Iris. The last time Iris saw Maddy was a bit over a year and a half ago, when she'd gotten married. Then her hair was black. Now it's a smooth honey-blond, worn long and wavy, old Hollywood style. She's dressed in black pants and a black T-shirt, black flats.

The women embrace, and Iris asks, "Is Nola here?" Maddy's seven-year-old daughter.

"She's taking a walk with Link and his dog," Maddy says. "I'm sorry to barge in on you like this without warning, but—"

"Oh, please, you know you're always welcome. It's your house! Is Matthew out with the kids?"

Maddy hangs her head, crosses her arms. Then looking up, her blue eyes tearful, she says, "We're taking some time."

Iris nods slowly. "Want to talk about it?"

"Not now."

"Well . . . I have to make a cake. Want to help?"

Now Maddy smiles her radiant smile and Iris can't help but smile back.

"Aprons in the same place as Lucille kept them?" Maddy asks, and Iris says, "The aprons will be in the same place as Lucille kept them forever."

It's About Time

"I'm really glad it's my turn tonight," says Joanie. "I've been wanting to share something for a long time." She blows out, then takes in a deep breath.

"Wait," Toots says. "I want to get some coffee. Anyone else?"

"I'll have some," Dodie says, and Rosemary says, "I will, too, but it *must* be decaf. Is it decaf?"

"Yes, it's decaf," Toots says. "I made it for Joanie, and checked the can twice."

"Well, last time we were at your house you said it was decaf and it wasn't."

"Oh. Right. Because I put caffeinated in the decaf can."

"Why?"

"I don't remember. But this is one hundred percent decaf, honest."

"You know what?" Rosemary says. "I'll just have water. Do you have lemon slices?"

"Excuse me," Joanie says. "I have something I'd really

like to say. And I'd appreciate it if you all would stop fiddling around and let me talk."

Toots, who has risen out of her chair, sits back down.

"I mean, you can get your *coffee* . . . " Joanie says.

"Don't need it," Toots says. "I'm sorry, Joanie. I apologize. I know how it is when you have something that you
want to say, something that you're maybe even dying to
say, but you're sort of scared, too. Even though all of us
here have shared some *very* personal things. Like remember the time when Gretchen told us about—"

"That confession is over now," Gretchen says. "We are
done with that."

"Okay," Toots says. "But my point is that we have all
opened ourselves up here in this club. Except for Anne
and Leah. They were kind of stingy that way, weren't they?
Like their idea of a confession was to say they forgot to
send someone a birthday card. The rest of us have all said
things that really . . . I mean, you share it and—*wham!*—
it's out there. It can make you feel awfully vulnerable."

Joanie opens her mouth, but Toots keeps talking.

"Just remember that we are your friends, Joanie, and
I'm sure we all understand that it can be hard to say some
things."

"*Especially* if someone keeps *talk*ing," Gretchen says.

Toots splays her fingers out over her breastbone. "Well,
pardon me!"

"Did you get a manicure?" Dodie asks, squinting across

the table at Toots. "Did you get that gel polish I told you about?"

Joanie stands. "I'm leaving. You all just stay here and enjoy yourselves. Lock the door when you leave."

"Wait!" Toots says. "Wait." She sighs. "I'm sorry. I really am. Please don't go. I'll be quiet. We all will. We yield the floor."

Joanie sits back down and folds her hands on the table. "Okay. I want to start by talking about when my husband cheated on me. I never gave you the details about that."

Silence at the table.

"I had been suspicious for a long time, but I guess I didn't *really* want to know. I just went to my job at the library every day, and came home every night and made dinner. Watched TV with him. Finally, though, I couldn't take it anymore. One Saturday morning at breakfast I asked him outright, 'Are you having an affair with Tammy Stuckmeyer?' She was someone he worked with; they traveled together. And he got all wide-eyed and denied it up and down. So I knew he was. And I just said, 'Okay,' and that night he took me out to dinner to my favorite restaurant, a place he otherwise never wanted to go. And my heart was sinking lower and lower the whole time we were there. My stomach hurt so bad I could hardly eat. I kept looking at him and thinking, 'You have been lying to me for so long.' And also I was thinking that I was too fat and my nose was ugly and I should have always worn a little foundation, I should have put highlights in my hair, I should have been wittier, more fun, and more *carefree*.

"The next day, I got . . . Well, I'm just going to go ahead and say what I believe happened. I got an infusion of strength from the spirit of my daddy, who thought I was God's gift. I got mad instead of sad and I called a private investigator. But he was so expensive, and I thought, 'Oh, what do I need him for anyway? I'll just go and research how those guys work and do the spying myself, and then, if I'm right, I'll get a divorce.'

"I rented a car so Kevin wouldn't recognize it, and I drove to his office at five that night, and waited for him to come out. He'd said he had a dinner meeting—he was having dinner meetings to beat the band at that time. He'd call me at the last minute to say he wasn't coming home. 'So sorry. Meeting. And don't wait up.' And me with the roast beef ready to come out of the oven and the potatoes mashed and the gravy just right. I'd say, 'Oh, okay then. Well, have a nice dinner! I love you!' My God. I'm so embarrassed to admit that."

Gretchen starts to say something and Joanie holds up her hand. "Let me just finish.

"I followed him after he came out, a car length back, and it was easier than I thought it would be. He drove to a townhouse and I saw him go in without knocking. I sat in the car for about fifteen minutes, like they said to do in *The Private Investigator's Handbook*. Or maybe it was in one of the other books I looked at. You really can find everything in books! Anyway, after I waited fifteen minutes, pretending I was on my phone so as not to attract any attention, I got out of the car and I walked right into the townhouse. It was very quiet, and then I heard sounds coming from upstairs. I thought of calling out his name, but no, I wanted to catch him right in the act. And I knew from the sounds that they were in the act. I knew those sounds, I knew *his* sounds, anyway. He . . . he used to . . .”

She stops talking and presses her fingers to her mouth, and Gretchen murmurs, “Oh, sweetheart.”

Joanie dabs her napkin at her eyes. But then she uses a mirthful, holding-back tone to say, “He used to go like this when he was coming: ‘*Honey. Honey. Oh, honey-honey-honey-honey, OOOOUGH!’* ” She bursts out laughing and all the other women do, too.

“Boy, that felt good!” Joanie says. “Anyway. I went up to the bedroom where the sounds were coming from and I barged in and . . . Well. You know. She’s naked. Flushed. Her hair all messed up. Him still inside her, and he turns around and I take a photo and I say, ‘Hello. Don’t come home. Not tonight and not ever again. The next time you hear from me will be through a lawyer. And I’m changing the locks as soon as I get home.’

“I went home and called a locksmith. And after the guy left, I wept hard. *Howled.* And then I made myself a big fat martini with about a thousand olives, I put it in my favorite Snoopy coffee mug, and I put on Beethoven’s Violin Sonata Number 3 really loud, I mean *really* loud. The next day I called Susie Keener, who, as some of you may know, is a lawyer who has a reputation for being formidable."

"Killer Keener," Toots says.

"Yes, I wanted the house. And as you all know, I got it. And I got something else more important, and that's what I really want to tell you about.

"Now, I know I have a reputation for being kind of rigid sometimes. Oftentimes, I guess. I mean, if I'm sitting with you at a restaurant and the salt and pepper shakers don't line up, why, I'm going to make them line up. I know it gets on people's nerves. It gets on *my* nerves. It's like some of us create our own prisons for ourselves, we fall into ways of being that we feel we can't change.

"But I was reading a book a few weeks ago—I like to read first thing in the morning these days, with my coffee. So I was reading the book and I went to take a sip of coffee and I spilled on the book. I got all upset: 'Now look! I ruined the book! Now I'll have to buy another one!' But I calmed down and kept on reading, and the next day, I kind of liked how the page had swollen a little in that spot where I'd spilled the coffee, I liked the tan outline. I liked how it felt beneath my fingers.

"I had never eaten when I was reading, but I started doing that. I got toast crumbs stuck in between two pages, I got a mustard stain on the bottom of another page, and I got a rip in the jacket and repaired it with Scotch tape. And, you know, the book became more lovable to me.

Lovable and comfortable and *mine*. I began dog-earing pages to indicate where I left off. I underlined passages I liked with whatever was closest: pen, pencil, Magic Markers, once even lipstick."

"Oh, my," Toots says. "You really went to the dark side. What book was it?"

"It was *The Bookshop of the Broken Hearted.* Robert Hillman. Beautiful book. You told me about it a while back, Gretchen. And you all know how I used to feel about people defacing books, but listen: It made it my book. It was me being me. I beat the hell out of that book, and it's now the one that I love the best. It's like it served as the revelation of Joanie Benson, as though I'd become my favorite toy from when I was a girl, the Visible Woman. The book is full of me. I can smell myself in it. I can see what resonates with me. When I finished it, I put it face-out on my bookshelf. If I ever read it again, and I think I will, I can come to the mustard stain and remember the day when it rained so hard the water ran down my windows like the house was going through a car wash, and I ate a baloney-and-mustard sandwich for lunch. All those marks I made in the book are . . . well, they're notes on a life. On my life. And they're important.

"Do you all know about Samuel Pepys? His diary of the unremarkable?"

"Didn't I just read an interview with him in the paper?" Dodie asks.

"No, he lived in the 1600s," Joanie says. "And people at

the time just *devoured* that book. I've begun carrying around something he wrote. Want to hear it?"

"Yes!" they all say.

Joanie reaches into her purse and pulls out a page from a yellow legal pad. She unfolds it and reads:

Strange to see how a good dinner and feasting reconciles everybody.

Mighty proud I am that I am able to have a spare bed for my friends.

Music and woman I cannot but give way to, whatever my business is.

Saw a wedding in the church. It was strange to see what delight we married people have to see these poor fools decoyed into our condition.

As happy a man as any in the world, for the whole world seems to smile upon me!

I find my wife hath something in her gizzard, that only waits an opportunity of being provoked to bring up; but I will not, for my content-sake, give it.

She looks up, smiling. "So, see? Turns out I'm glad I'm divorced! And I know it wasn't exactly right to walk in on them that way, but I'm glad I did it! This is a confession, but I'm not one bit sorry."

"Hmm," Toots says. "I'll bet a lot of us could confess things we did wrong that we'd do again."

"Like what?" Dodie asks.

Toots pats primly at her mouth with her napkin. "Not my turn," she says.

Welcome to the Club

At seven-thirty that evening, Maddy comes along with Iris to deliver the Black Cake to Joanie's club. In the car, she tells Iris she remembers Joanie from when she was head librarian. "I always liked her," Maddy says. "She was so kind."

"She is kind," Iris says. "She's taken a couple of my classes and she's always the first one to help anyone who needs it."

When they pull up outside the house, Iris tells Maddy to sit still until she comes around to take the cake off her lap. It's rather nice-looking, and smells heavenly. Iris brought along some whipped cream, too, in part to compensate for delivering the cake so late; it took a long time indeed to make it.

Halfway down the walk, they hear the loud sound of women laughing. "What kind of club is this?" Maddy asks, and Iris says, "I think it's a book club."

The door has been left ajar, and a note taped to it says, IRIS, COME ON IN!

The women are now engrossed in quiet conversation and Iris motions to Maddy to follow her down the hall to the kitchen. She'll just drop the cake and whipped cream off and, on the way out, signal to Joanie that it's there.

She and Maddy are just outside the dining room when they hear a woman say, "It was a first date. I can't call him for a second date when I farted like that on the first! In the car! It was so awful. Neither one of us said anything. He just cleared his throat and rolled down the window a tiny bit. And I turned up the radio. Like that might help!"

Maddy and Iris look at each other, and then Joanie spies them and says, "Oh, look, girls! Iris is here. Iris Winters? You remember her: Winters Baking School? She brought that complicated cake I was telling you about for dessert. Come on in and say hello, Iris. And who . . . ? Is that Maddy Harris with you? Maddy! Come on in! Sit down and have some cake before you go. We had a couple of no-shows; Anne and Leah had something going on in their retirement home." Joanie points to the two empty chairs. "I'll bet you're dying to see what that cake tastes like."

"I am curious," Iris says, putting the cake on the table and then sitting down. "What book are you discussing?"

"Oh, this is not a book club," Karen Lundgren says. "Newwwwwww."

"What kind of a club is it?" Iris asks.

No one says anything. But then Joanie comes in with a cake server, plates, and forks. She slices the cake into even pieces and passes it out. Then she says, "Okay, Iris, I heard you ask what kind of club this is. I will confess that we call it Confession Club."

Silence.

"We confess things to one another. Things that we did wrong or that we're ashamed of."

"*Joanie . . .* " Rosemary says. Rosemary is wearing a pretty print tie blouse and has a pastel sweater draped over her shoulders. She has on many bracelets, sparkly earrings. She has highlighted, chin-length hair worn in a loose perm, and she is wearing very skillfully applied makeup. Iris thinks she looks like a mannequin brought to life.

"*What,* Rosemary?" says Joanie. "Talking about things you're ashamed of is nothing to be ashamed of."

"I think it sounds sort of wonderful," Iris says.

"And therapeutic," Maddy adds. "And anyway, isn't listening to things like that what good friends do for one another all the time?"

"Not often enough, actually," Joanie says. And then, licking her fork, "Jeez. This is good."

Toots leans forward to say loudly, "I run things here just like I run the town council meetings. We take things seriously, and we go into them in depth. Each week, one person shares, and we almost always spend the whole time on just her."

"Can I join?" Iris asks. She means it as a joke, but now that she's said it, she realizes she is kind of serious.

No one answers. Joanie sits wide-eyed across from her, her mouth full, and Iris bets she knows what she's remembering: Iris saying to her, *Someday I will call upon you to do a service for me. . . .* She's about to tell Joanie that she's only kidding, but then Maddy doubles down and says, "I'd like to join, too. For a few weeks, anyway. I'll be here for at least a few weeks." She looks over at Iris, shrugs.

Karen, the minister's wife, says, "Wait. Are you in your fifties, Iris?" She sounds very excited. She pushes up on the sleeves of her striped sweater like she's getting ready to wash dishes.

"Close. Couple of months."

Karen looks around the table. "You guys. Anne and Leah are going to drop out, they're going to move to Arizona in a month. And we don't have anyone in her fifties."

"Excuse me," Rosemary says. "I am fifty-eight."

"Yeah," Karen says, "but you said you're going to say you're sixty and get it over with. So I'm going to count you as being in your sixties. And, Maddy, you're what, in your twenties, right?"

"Right."

"Well, see?" Karen says. "If we let them in, we'll have the twenties, thirties, forties, fifties, sixties, and seventies represented!"

Gretchen says, "I'll bet we could get on cable TV. They could film us at my store, and that way no one would have to worry about her private space being invaded. Grace Haddock got on cable TV for her poetry and her poetry isn't even good!"

"I like her poetry," says Dodie, delicately plucking something off her tongue. "Why don't you like it?" She's wearing a very dramatic white blouse with the collar turned up. Iris thinks she could pass as a faded movie star. That red lipstick!

"I think what we need to talk about is whether we'd like to admit two new people," Joanie says.

Toots leaps into action. "There is a motion on the floor to admit two new members to our club, which I second even though technically I can't, as chair. Is there any discussion?"

"Well, this is just happening all too fast for me," Rosemary says, the color high in her face. She pulls her sweater off her shoulders and lays it across her lap.

"That's why we have discussion," Toots says.

Rosemary speaks quietly, looking down as though she is addressing her bosom. "I think we need to talk privately first."

"It's okay," Iris says, and starts to rise out of her chair. But Toots, who is sitting next to her, puts her hand over Iris's: *Stay.*

"Rosemary," Toots says, "we're not discussing whether to bomb North Korea. We're talking about admitting two new women to our little club in our little town."

"Which would probably be good for us," says Dodie.

"We need some new blood! I've thought that for some time, but there wasn't any room. Now, with Leah and Anne leaving, we could use two more. I say it's providential. Let's let these two in!" She coughs spectacularly into her napkin. "Excuse me."

"I think I get what Rosemary is concerned about, though," says Gretchen. "A lot of what we say here is really personal. Sensitive."

"How about if we have it be on a trial basis?" Joanie asks. "Maddy and Iris can come to the next meeting, and we'll see how it goes. If anyone is uncomfortable— including them—the deal is off. How's that?"

Silence, but for the scraping of Gretchen's fork against the cake plate. "Do you have the recipe for this?" she asks Joanie, and Joanie says, "Trust me, you don't want it."

"Any other discussion?" Toots asks. No one says anything, and Toots says, "Is there a motion to vote?"

"I move to vote," says Maddy.

Toots looks at her. "As you are not yet in the club, you can't make such a motion."

"I move to vote," says Joanie.

"All in favor of admitting two new people?" Toots asks.

"Trying *out*," Rosemary says, and Toots says, "All in favor of *trying out* Maddy and Iris?"

Everyone in the club except for Rosemary raises her hand.

"Opposed?" Toots says, and Rosemary hesitates, then says, "Oh, all right, I'll vote 'for.'"

"Unanimous!" says Toots. "We will try out these two next time we meet."

Taking their cue, Iris and Maddy get up, and on their way out the door, Rosemary rushes over to them. "I'm sorry," she says. "I don't mean to seem inhospitable. But when it's my turn, my confession is . . ."

"I understand completely," Iris says.

"Me, too," Maddy says. "I respect your honesty."

"Well, it has to do with lust. Which, as you may know, is one of the seven deadly sins."

"Uh-huh," says Iris.

Now no one says anything until Rosemary says, "That's all I can say. I hope you understand."

"We do," says Maddy, and Rosemary presses her hand to her heart, offers a sad smile, and closes the door after them.

Back in the car, Maddy says, "What do you think? An affair? A slip?"

"I guess we'll find out," Iris says.

Maddy looks out the window. "So, *can* I stay with you for a few weeks? I confess I wasn't sure I was staying here that long until I heard myself say so."

"Of course!"

"I'll arrange for Nola to finish her class work here. There are just a couple of weeks left, and Nola has always wanted to try home schooling."

"Okay."

Maddy sighs. "I love this town. Isn't that stupid?"

"Not to me," Iris says.

When they arrive back home, they go into the kitchen for a cup of tea. Iris tells Maddy, "It's great that you're here; I could use your help. I want to go and cut lilacs out in the country tomorrow morning. Will you help me by doing a little prep work for my eleven o'clock class so I can take my time getting the flowers?"

"Absolutely. What are you teaching?"

"Super-Fast Sticky Buns."

"Oh, I love them! Lucille made them every Sunday for Arthur and me."

"So you know how to make them?"

"In my sleep. *Nola* can make them."

As if on cue, the little girl comes banging in the kitchen door from having been next door, where she was staying with Link and his parents while Maddy and Iris delivered the cake. She's wearing a red corduroy skirt, a pink blouse with birds on it, polka-dotted tights, and cowgirl boots. Her ponytail has slid halfway down her head, and her bangs are sticking straight up. "Hi, Iris!" she says. "I'll bet you guys were just talking about me."

"What happened to your bangs?" Maddy asks.

The girl presses gently on them. "Did you know this happens if you put egg white on things? Link taught me. He's a scientist. He's got a microscope and also a chemistry set. He's going to cure cancer and win the Doorbell Prize."

"You mean . . . Nobel?"

"Yeah, that's it." She sighs. "I'm getting sleepy and I

hate sleeping so much. Why can't we just stay up all the time? We miss everything!"

"Maybe Link will figure out a way to help us stay up all the time," Maddy says. "But for now—"

"I know, I know," Nola says. "Put on my pajamas. Wash my face. Brush my teeth, yada yada, yada."

She leaves the kitchen and clomps upstairs.

"*She's* gotten older," Iris says.

"She was born old," Maddy says.

Lilac Time

✥

The next morning, it's raining again. Iris stands at her bedroom window, watching the birds that have sought shelter
in the trees and beneath the eaves of her house. They are
subdued, watchful, and there's something so cozy about
them huddling down this way that she is tempted to go
back to bed. But she wants the lilacs at that old farmhouse,
and she needs to get home in time for her class. So she
quickly washes up, forgoes any makeup, and dresses in
khaki cargo pants, a black T-shirt, and high-top sneakers.
The sneakers are black glitter, a kind of joke shoe she had
at the clothing consignment shop she used to own in Boston, but they've come in handy for days like today.

On the way out of town, Iris uses the drive-through at
Caff-fiend for a large coffee, double cream, no sugar.
What is it that's so pleasant about getting morning coffee
out, she wonders, when it's so little trouble for most people to make it at home? She isn't sure—the camaraderie?

The reassurance of seeing that you aren't the only one up and at 'em? The way we prize individuality but nonetheless find comfort in sameness? The filing of citizenry out from coffee shops always reminds Iris of cattle coming out of a barn in the morning, in their slow, blinking line. Not the most flattering of images, but for her, it's calming, suggesting a kind of optimism about at least one thing in the world. A new day. A new start.

When she reaches the county road on which she saw the abandoned farmhouse, she turns off NPR, the better to pay attention. She doesn't remember exactly where it was, but the huge bank of dark-purple lilacs in front of it will be hard to miss. She's gone about two miles when she sees the brilliant stand, a silent paean to spring. Some boughs are weighted down so much by their wet blossoms that they are touching the ground.

She pulls into the rutted dirt driveway, bumpy enough to make it feel like her fillings are rattling. A rusted black mailbox at the edge of the driveway lists to the side, as if pulling back out of her way and welcoming her intention to pilfer. The rain has let up to a fine drizzle now. She can get the flowers and with any luck be out of here before the sky opens again—the forecast is brutal, especially for late this afternoon.

She gets her scissors out of the glove compartment and slides them into the side pocket of her pants. From the floor of the backseat, she carefully lifts out one of the three big containers she brought along—thick plastic buckets in which thirty pounds of flour and sugar are regularly delivered to her door. They had been empty, but the water she added halfway up makes them surprisingly heavy again. She rests the first bucket on the ground before gripping the handle with both hands to hike it up, grunting. Then she does a modified duck walk over to the bushes.

"Need any help?" she hears, and, startled, drops the bucket. Before her is a good-looking man, maybe early sixties, in faded jeans and a blue work shirt, and his smile is so disarming she tables her fear.

The man reaches forward to stand the bucket upright. "Sorry I scared you. Now you've spilled your water." He looks up at the sky. "Looks like more is on the way, though. Here for the lilacs, I presume?"

She pulls the scissors from her pocket as though to confess, but also is aware—as she thinks the man might be—that they could serve as a weapon, should she need one.

"Do you live here?" she asks. "I'm so sorry. I thought this place was abandoned, or I never would have . . ." She gestures toward the bucket.

"Yes, I'm here for a while. But you can take the lilacs. Want some help? I could hold the bucket for you."

She considers this, then says, "I have to tell you, I was planning on taking a lot of them. I have two more buckets in the car."

"Knock yourself out." He grabs the bucket and stands beside a bush, watching her. Iris glances over at her car— a short distance away, easy to run to.

"I'm a perfectly nice guy," he says, "but if you'd be more comfortable, I can go back inside and read the dictionary."

Iris laughs. He does have a very kind face. "No, I'd actually appreciate the help."

The man points at the lower boughs. "These are easy. But the ones up higher are fuller. Closer to the sun, I guess, is why."

"That's always the way," Iris says. "The ones hardest to reach are always the best."

"You may be interested to know that I can still climb trees," the man says.

"Hmm," she says. "And you may be interested to know that I cannot. So, isn't this lucky for me?"

"For me, too," the man says. Iris wants to ask why, but doesn't.

They work quietly for a while, Iris snipping as she moves slowly around the bushes. As promised, the man holds the bucket she collects the stems in. At one point he says, "Hey, look at that!" and indicates a particularly lush grouping of blossoms, higher up. "You want those?" he asks.

"That would be great." She hands him the scissors, then immediately regrets it.

But he only stands on his tiptoes and reaches up to take hold of the branch. He's remarkably gentle, doing this. And she thinks his hands are beautiful: he has the long fingers of a pianist or a surgeon or an artist. His shirt rises to reveal his stomach as he reaches up higher to cut, and Iris looks away, then back. Apparently, sometimes when you feel yourself done with something, you're not done with it at all. Inside her, a specific longing stirs.

The sun peeks out and they both look up at the sky.

"Think it's going to stop?" Iris asks, and he says, "Nah. False hope." He puts the flowers in her bucket. "Good ones," he says, handing her back the scissors.

She looks down at the blossoms, then up at him. "Thanks a bunch. So to speak."

"Can I tell you something? You're really a beautiful woman. No offense."

"None taken. Not at my age."

"What's your age?"

"Coming into my fifties."

He nods.

"How about you?" Iris asks.

"Sixty-six."

"Really?"

"Really."

"Well, you certainly don't look sixty-six."

"Lots of fresh air."

His voice is steady, and youthful with its undercurrent of energy. There's none of the sighing or resignation that she often hears in the voices of older people—that, if truth be told, she sometimes hears in herself.

"I guess if you really don't mind, I'll fill the other buckets," she says, looking over at the car.

"Let's do it," he says, and lifts the full bucket to carry it to the car.

After Iris resumes cutting and putting the lilacs into the buckets he brought out for her, he says, "Well, what do you think? Should we exchange names?"

She extends her hand. "Iris Winters."

"I'm John," he says.

"John . . . ?"

He only smiles.

"Do you have a last name?"

"Loney."

"Are you Irish?"

"I'm afraid I am." Then, putting on the lilt: "But you won't hold a man's DNA against him now, will yeh?"

"What do you do?" Iris asks.

"I used to refinish furniture. But now . . . well, now I would say I'm in the business of waiting for things to come along. And you?"

"I used to own a consignment store in Boston. But I live in Mason now, and I teach baking classes." She bends to cut more lilacs from a low branch.

"Are you happy?"

She straightens and faces him, flustered. "I . . . Do you mean, am I happy teaching baking?"

"That, too." He takes the flowers from her and adds them to the bucket.

"I am happy teaching baking. And otherwise, I would say I'm happy enough."

There is a loud crack of thunder, followed immediately by a flash of lightning. Then again. The thunder is so loud Iris can feel the reverberations in her chest. The last two buckets of flowers are barely half-full. She looks at her car, then at John.

"Come in if you'd like to," he says, and starts toward the house. Over his shoulder, his thick silver hair obscuring one eye, he adds, "I've got tea and graham crackers, and for entertainment I can recite the Gettysburg Address. When the rain lets up again, we'll fill those buckets fast as Jimmy's ashes."

Iris stands there. Then she calls after him, "What does *that* mean?"

"No idea," he shouts. "My mother used to say it." He turns around. "Oh, come on, then, Iris. I've got Hershey bars, too. Come around back; the front door's stuck."

She doesn't move, and he walks back over to her, his shoulders hunched against the rain that has begun again. "If you're nervous about coming in, we can stay outside and continue the conversation. I'll go and get us chairs, and we'll take our chances with the lightning."

Iris laughs, then decides that a killer would not reveal that the front door was stuck. Nor would a killer cut flowers so gently. Probably. At any rate, she's going to take a chance. She does have her scissors back in her pocket. She'll sit near the door, and if she needs to, she'll run out fast as Jimmy's ashes.

When Iris crosses the threshold into the kitchen, she

sees a Formica table in the middle of the room, with four evenly spaced chairs around it, a braided rug beneath. At the center of the table is a coffee can full of wildflowers. There's a fat red candle decorated with dusty holly and berries off to one side, burned down low. There is also a small pile of books, and on top—she can see it from here, even in the dimness—is an old hardback American College Dictionary, the pale-blue binding frayed. There's something deliciously inviting about it. Maybe John wasn't kidding about reading it. Iris uses her computer whenever she needs to look up a word, but she misses leafing through the delicate pages of a dictionary, trying to remember to use the guide words Mrs. Murray taught her about in elementary school; she misses, too, coming across incidental words that end up being as useful as the ones whose meanings she sought.

"Come and sit," John says.

Iris lowers herself into a chair, her hands in her lap. She's damp from the rain, and she shivers.

"Cold?" he asks.

"I'm okay."

"Wait there."

He disappears into another room and returns with a faded quilt, which he drapes over her shoulders. "Better?"

"Better."

She pulls the quilt tighter around herself and looks around the kitchen. A few mismatched dishes are neatly stacked on one counter: plates, mugs, glasses, and a small cast-iron pan. There is also a spatula, a few forks and spoons, and a paring knife with a chipped red handle. On another counter are jugs of water, plastic bags of what look like trail mix, cans of soup, Honey Nut Cheerios, a big box of Lipton tea, and a wooden bowl holding an apple, an orange, and a spotted banana. There's a box from Sugarbutter bakery, the twine undone. She wonders what he got.

The cupboards are hanging crookedly on the wall; they look like you could blow them down. A few missing windowpanes have been filled in with cardboard. There is no stove, only a space where it used to be. There is no refrigerator, either, but there is a beat-up cooler in the space where it must have been. A mop and broom are in another corner. The place is comfortable, despite its limitations, and though Iris has now figured out that the man is squatting, she doesn't mind being here with him. It's interesting, being here.

John digs in the cooler and produces an iced tea. "This okay?"

"It's fine, thank you."

"I'd offer you hot tea but I can't build a fire in the rain."

"Next time," she says, and the words surprise her—they just leaped out.

But, "Yes, next time," he says, and it's as natural as if she had said "Thank you" and he had said "You're welcome."

He sits at the table opposite her, empty-handed. "Where's *your* tea?" Iris asks. The rain is beating down so hard on the roof now that she must raise her voice to be heard.

"Oh, that was the last one."

"I'm sorry. We could have shared. Now I've drunk from it, though."

"*Kissing the glass*, we call it, drinking after someone else. I don't mind it, but I had a tea just before you came; I don't need anything just now."

He sets out four squares of graham crackers on a plate and holds it out to her. She takes one and bites in. "Delicious," she says, and she means it; they've not gone soft from the humidity. She can't remember the last time she had a graham cracker, plain. On a rainy day. Sitting across from a man with a bit of stubble and blue eyes that seem to change color depending on the light. Blue, then greenish, then back again. "Hershey bar?" he asks.

"No, thank you. This is fine." Actually, she wouldn't mind; she loves Hershey bars. But he has so little.

He rubs his arms. "It is a bit cold in here."

"Yes. And I have your blanket." She starts to take it off, and he says, "Keep it—I'll get my jacket."

He goes into the other room again and returns wearing a military field jacket. The fabric is darker where patches have been removed.

He smiles at the unasked question in her face. "An awful lot of homeless people are vets. But then I'll bet you knew that."

"Are you?"

"What, a vet?"

"Yes."

"I am. I went to Vietnam for a year that felt like a thousand. And I'm homeless, too. Have been off and on—mostly on—for a long time now. Although for the time being . . ." He gestures widely. "I guess I'm not so *very* homeless."

The rain suddenly stops, and now it's the quiet that's loud.

"I think we should get the rest of your flowers," John says. "You know that your house will reek of lilacs, don't you? You'll be able to *taste* that smell."

"That's fine with me."

He pushes his chair away from the table, starts to stand, then stops and leans in closer to her. "Do you sing, Iris?"

"Not well, but yes. Sure."

"Because I found a perfectly good guitar at the dump yesterday. A Gibson B-25. Missing a D string is all."

"Easy to fix," says Iris.

"Easy enough if . . . Is there a music store in town?"

"No, next town over, a few miles east." She doesn't offer to take him, and he doesn't ask.

"Be right back," John says. When he returns, he's holding the guitar. It looks like it's in good shape. *The things people throw away!* Iris thinks. She'd like to go to the dump, too. She does have an eye for what's worth salvaging, or her consignment store never would have done so well. She can spin the word *vintage* with the best of them.

And she has always had a great deal of appreciation for the odd adventure. Her favorite date in high school was the time Rob Levinson told her to wear old clothes and they'd explore storm drains and then run down hills. He was president of the drama club, and he was a wonderful actor. He had an enigmatic but friendly manner, and a great wit. She still thinks of that, sometimes, how that boy was the kind of boy she should have been with, not the jocks she normally dated. When Rob dropped her off that night, he said, "You know you belong with us, don't you?" He never asked her out again, though. And Iris didn't "chase" him, as her mother would have called it. Girls didn't go after boys. Girls waited.

John strums the guitar and begins to sing, "*When I die / don't put me in the ground / Put my ashes in the ashtray / and drive me around.*" He sings the word *around* like James Taylor does, with a long *a.*

Iris laughs. "Did you write that?"

"Nope. A genius songwriter named Warren Nelson wrote that."

"There are no ashtrays in cars anymore."

"More's the pity. But the song's still good. All his songs are good. I met him in a bar, a long time ago. He was wearing a leather vest and a black derby and I told him I liked his hat. He said, 'Everybody I meet tells me that.' His band was playing the bar that night, they had just finished setting up, and Warren thought he'd have a beer before going back to the hotel. I had one with him. I had just gotten a divorce and I was miserable. 'Are you married?' I asked him. And he said, 'Yup, to a tree.' And then he explained that a woman he'd loved realized at some point that he would never want to get married. That was a disappointment to her, but she understood his need for freedom. She told him he might not want to get married but he had a strong need for commitment, and he said he guessed that was right. She said he should marry a tree, and she performed the ceremony herself. And then the two of them consummated the marriage, because the tree couldn't do that part. 'What happened to that woman?' I asked him. And he said, 'Lost her. She got married to someone else.' He raised his glass, then. 'Here's to the ones who got away,' he said. 'Here's to the ones who got away whom we wish would come back.'"

John stares at the floor for a long moment, then looks up to study her features as though he's drawing her. He takes his time, and the way his eyes roam her face makes it feel like he's touching her. Finally, "Are you married, Iris?" he asks.

"Divorced."

"For how long?"

"Twelve years."

"Are you over it?"

"You ask very personal questions!"

"Yes, I know I do. But are you? Over it?"

She smiles.

"Ah, we none of us ever are, are we?" he says. "Even

when you want to leave everything behind, something remains. Burr in the pants leg, pain in the heart." He stands, leans the guitar carefully against the wall. "Let's go out and get more lilacs."

Iris looks at her watch. She supposes she should get going. But she doesn't want to leave. She wants to call Maddy and tell her to teach the class so that she can stay here and listen to a handsome man play a five-string guitar.

"I believe I'm owed a recitation of the Gettsyburg Address," she says.

"Oh, I'm saving that for last," he says. "Just before you drive away, I'll recite it. And all the way home, you can think about it."

After they finish filling the buckets with lilacs, John puts them in Iris's car. He opens her door for her to get in and she rolls the window down. "Thanks again, John. For everything."

He puts his hands on the car door and leans his head in so that his face is close to hers. Not close enough to make her uncomfortable, but close enough. He smells like hay. My God, his eyes are beautiful. He recites the Gettysburg Address, stone-faced, while Iris giggles. But then she stops laughing and really listens to the eloquent and still relevant words, maybe for the first time in her life.

John straightens. "I took it upon myself to learn that in fourth grade," he says. "My teacher took me straight to the principal's office when I recited it for her. I thought I was in trouble, but she just wanted me to recite it for him, too. Then nothing would do but that he had to make me a little certificate with a gold star on it. Listen, Iris, Iris Winters. Would it be all right if I called you sometime?"

"I . . . Yes. Do you have a phone? Do you want to go and get it and put in my number?"

"I'll remember it."

She tells him her number and tries to ignore the voice of the vestigial high schooler who still lives inside her saying, "Well, *ob*viously he doesn't *really* want your number!" She waves goodbye then, and drives slowly through the muddy little lakes that have formed in the long driveway. It's beautiful outside. It's as though the edges of the world have been lightly erased, and everything is infused with a violet light: the sky, the droplets that hang from the tips of leaves, the mesh of tall weeds at the side of the road, even the road itself. Then, as the color begins to fade, she realizes it was a trick of the eye, a kind of saturation that occurred from looking so deeply at all those purple lilacs. But it was wonderful, that false vision, an unconscious surrender to seeing things another way.

Just as she is ready to turn out of the driveway, her phone rings. Maddy, no doubt: Where *are* you? But no, UNKNOWN CALLER, the screen says. Probably someone wanting to sign up a whole group for a class—they usually called first, to make sure there would be room.

She answers and hears John say, "Iris Winters. John Loney. Do you remember me?"

She laughs. "Oh, come for dinner on Saturday night, why don't you?" She gives him the address.

"What time?" he asks.

"Six. Shall I pick you up?"

"I believe you already have," he says, "but I'd love a ride, too. I'll be ready, with my hair wet-combed."

"Do you have any allergies?"

"Just to bad company and good luck."

Oh, those Irishmen, Iris thinks, after she hangs up.

Well, guess what. Iris is Irish, too. One-quarter, anyway. And that one-quarter of herself now awakens, yawns mightily, and stretches—fists in the air and arms as straight as asparagus stalks.

Iris decides something. She is going to iron her white cotton dress with lace at the yoke, because it is spring on the way to summer, and she is amid all the green and growing things. She is going to buy a red bicycle and paint white polka dots on it. She is going to affix a basket onto the handlebars and fill it every day with incidental offerings, which abound. She is going to unearth her one slim volume of Yeats. She knows she still has it.

She stretches back against the car seat, thinking, *Homeless.* That's what John is, a homeless man, though with enough charm and good hygiene to obviate the usual stigma. She recalls the homeless people she used to see in the library in Boston. One day she sat near a man in the lobby who was sleeping in the sun like a cat, one leg up on a banged-up suitcase that she presumed held his necessities. He did not have the peaceful expression that most people do in sleep, though; his weariness seemed evident even in his eyebrows. It was as though he knew the repose he was enjoying now wouldn't go far. Why would it, when these people were constantly subjected to being awakened, when nothing in their lives was secure?

She had a notion about trying to help that man, somehow. But no ideas came to her. She had sat watching him for a while, then decided that the best thing she might do was let him sleep. She slipped a twenty-dollar bill in his front shirt pocket and tiptoed away. She'd heard often enough that one should not give money to the homeless, that one should instead direct them to a shelter where they might get help. But a woman she worked with who routinely gave money to people on the street said something else. "Isn't it hard enough for them to even ask?" she said. "Do I really need to tell them what to do with their lives when I know absolutely nothing about them? I just feel an obligation to try to help in some way. What else can I do to help someone?"

Maybe date him, Iris thinks. And then, with a delicious shiver, she thinks, *What is happening here?*

Breakfast at the Henhouse

✦

At ten-thirty in the morning, Nola and Maddy have finished prepping for Iris's class. Earlier, they baked a batch of Super-Fast Sticky Buns to serve as an example, and the kitchen smells of cinnamon and butter. Maddy set out the equipment that would be necessary to teach the simple recipe, and Nola drew daisies on the place cards and carefully printed the names of all the students. Just as Maddy looks at her watch, wondering where Iris is, her phone rings—Iris apologizing for how long she was gone and saying she would be there in about ten minutes. Maddy wants not to be in the way when Iris teaches the class, so she asks Nola if she would like to go to Polly's Henhouse for a late breakfast.

"I ate breakfast," Nola says. "Remember?"

"Yes," Maddy says, "but you didn't eat very much."

"I know. I was in a hurry." Nola says this as though it's an anomaly, when in fact it's how the girl usually eats: head down, minimal conversation, maximum speed in clearing what she'll eat from her plate. The problem is, she doesn't ever eat much, and so she's always hungry early for the next meal. It's apparently useless to try to change her; nothing Maddy has tried so far has worked.

"Can I have lunch there?" Nola asks.

"If they're serving it this early."

"I hope they are because I want the Itty-Bitty Burger with Teepee Fries. Link told me about it. You get a teepee made of French fries, and you get to wreck it. And *eat* it!"

"Sounds great!"

"You can have one," Nola says. "But wait, you might have to be a kid."

"We'll figure something out. I might want the Crybaby Omelet." Lots of jalapeños in that one.

"Can we walk there?"

Maddy looks askance at her.

"I know it's raining," the girl says, looking earnestly up at her mother. "But it will be fun. Can we?"

"Sometimes it is fun to walk in the rain, I agree," says Maddy. "But today there's thunder and lightning, so I think we'll drive."

They go out to the car under umbrellas that seem laughable against the force of the rain. Nola is chatty the whole way to the Henhouse: "Look! A dog with three legs! Oh. Wait. No, he has four. Whew, I was going to get a little bit sad for him."

"Look! Those people painted their front door red! Can you do that? Can we do that?"

"Look! Doesn't that tree look like it has a grumpy face?"

"Hey, the rain stopped! I was saying inside, 'Rain, rain go away,' and it did!"

Maddy is grateful; she doesn't want to talk much. She's thinking about something. She's wondering where Matthew is right now, what he's doing. In the conversations they've had since she left for her visit to Mason, she's felt herself growing increasingly distant. She doesn't want to be that way, yet she is. She doesn't know what to tell him. She doesn't know what to tell herself.

And then, to make matters worse, she called her father last night to set up some time with him, and though he pretended to be glad, Maddy knew that he wasn't. She feels he will never get over blaming her for her mother's death, which happened just after Maddy was born; it's as though he can't separate the two events. "I can't help my feelings," he told her once, when she was still in high school, and she remembers thinking, *But you can help your behavior.*

Things didn't get much better when she got pregnant by a guy who couldn't dump her fast enough, nor did they improve after Nola was born. And then, after Maddy got married and moved to New York, the two of them became even more estranged. She had to put a note in her calendar to remember to check in with her father from time to time; he never initiated contact. She confronted him about that once and he apologized, but nothing changed.

If there was anything Maddy learned after Arthur and Lucille took her in as a pregnant teenager, it was that families don't have to be biological. She finds it hard to let go of the notion that you should matter to your father, though. It's hard to let go of that need, even if the fallout from the love he denied her as a child has insinuated itself into her, seemingly forever. She doesn't know if it's best to continue to see her father and try to get to a place of forgiveness, or to cross him off the list as simply toxic. She's heard people make the case for both sides.

The other night, when she and Iris were in the living room having a glass of wine before bed, Maddy told Iris that the only person she feels she has a clean relationship with is Nola.

"By 'clean' you mean . . . ?"

"Unfettered, you know? Just pure love."

"But what about Matthew?" Iris asked. "And Arthur? And Lucille?"

Maddy nodded. "I did love Arthur and Lucille. But they're gone now, and I . . ."

She fell silent, then said, "I do love Matthew. But it's a nervous love. Nola is the only person I can love without feeling like the floor might open beneath me. She's the only one that I think I love *right*." She looked over at Iris, feeling embarrassed, suddenly, for having revealed so much. "Do you know what I mean?"

Iris nodded. "Yes. And I want to tell you that I think the love you're able to give Nola is such a beautiful triumph.

You may not be able to see it yourself, but you've grown, Maddy. I see you as more open than you've ever been. I think it takes a long time to get over some things, especially if they happened when you were so young and vulnerable. Maybe you never get over them, but you can learn to work around them."

Iris leaned back against the sofa cushions, swirled the wine in her glass. "You know, I have my own problems opening up. I could blame it on my growing-up years or a kind of New England reticence, I suppose. But I've learned that blaming doesn't get you far. Self-reflection helps. Trying to change helps, too. But it's hard, Maddy, I'll give you that. It's hard, but I think it's worth it to try. Sometimes little successes here and there can all of a sudden . . . I don't know . . . consolidate, I guess, and you see that you really are a different person."

Driving down the familiar streets of Mason, Maddy realizes how much she has missed this town. The bullying she endured in high school was horrible, but there was an English teacher who made up for it—the very one who helped her become a photographer. And Matthew helped her with everything.

Living in New York City was thrilling at first, but something about it made Maddy feel as though she were sitting halfway off a chair: unbalanced and ill at ease. And lately it has begun to feel as though some veneer were wearing thin, and old ways of thinking have started coming back.

Never mind her success at the galleries where her photographs are shown, never mind the funny and interesting and intelligent friends she and Matthew spend time with. More and more often, she comes back from having spent an evening out with them and thinks, *Oh, thank goodness it's over.* That old fear reasserting itself, that feeling that if she spends too long with people, she will be *found out.* On those nights, she goes to bed and lies awake in the dark, a black space at her center expanding. She locks her hands together to hold on.

It's all broken glass inside me, she once wrote in her journal, when she was in high school. *I breathe, and I cut myself.* At least she's made some progress from that point of view. But she has a long way to go, and living in New York hasn't helped. *Maybe it's true that there's no place like home,* she thinks, pulling into the parking lot of the Henhouse. When she opens the car door, she can smell the bacon.

As soon as they come in the door of the restaurant, Monica Dawson, the owner, who is standing at the cash register, spots them. "Hey!" she says. "Either of you want to help in the kitchen after you eat?"

"I do!" says Nola.

"No?" Monica says.

"I do!" Nola says, louder.

"Well, okay, if nobody wants to unwrap those big blocks of butter for Roberto—"

"*I will do it!*" says Nola, and her voice practically bounces off the walls.

Monica grins.

One of the eighty-something men sitting at a table with his cronies says, "Anybody know when laryngitis season starts?"

Dinner Date

At five-thirty on Saturday evening, Iris inspects herself in the bathroom mirror one more time. She's wearing white jeans and a periwinkle-blue silk blouse, the sleeves rolled up, a few silver bangle bracelets, silver hoop earrings, sandals. It's still only May but the temperature was in the eighties today. She's lightly made up: mascara, pink lipstick. Her hair is freshly washed and loose around her face. No perfume. Just an instinct she had.

When she comes into the kitchen to tell Maddy and Nola that she'll be back with John in about forty minutes, she sees Nola kneeling on a kitchen chair, frosting the chocolate cupcakes she made "completely by herself." Maddy is standing by the window, leaning against the frame and looking out.

"Hey," Iris says.

Nola looks up. "Hi, Iris. You look pretty."

"Thank you, Nola."

Maddy turns around. "Wow, you *do* look pretty."

"Thank you! I just wanted to let you know that I'd be back by six. I guess we'll have the wine and cheese out on the front porch—what do you think? It's so nice out."

"Sure," Maddy says. "I'll pick some daffodils and put them out there. Then I'll finish the salad. I'll put the eggplant lasagna in the oven in about ten, fifteen minutes?"

"Perfect. I'll see you soon."

"Can I walk out with you?" Maddy asks, and then, "You okay, Nola?"

Nola nods in the springy, overenergetic way of children. "I only need to frost"—she stops to count—"three more. And then I'm going to put cherries on top. And then I'm done. But I *might* put chopped walnuts on there. Like glitter."

"That sounds great," Maddy says. "I'll be right back."

Iris had told Maddy only a few things about John. She described him as a man she ran into when she went to cut lilacs. A nice guy. So, you know, she invited him to dinner. Maddy had looked at her as though she were perfectly well aware that Iris was holding something back, but she wasn't going to press her. It wasn't like Maddy to press anyone. But now Iris thinks that Maddy may have a few questions after all.

Once they are outside, though, Maddy only says quietly, "I'm thinking of enrolling Nola in the Little Red School House for the summer. Do you know it?"

"I've seen it. I know people like it. But . . . are you sure?"

Maddy looks away, nods.

"So . . . you want to stay here that long?"

"I don't know. I might. If it's okay with you."

"Of course it's okay with me. But . . ." Iris looks at her watch. "I would love to talk more about this, Maddy. I just want to make sure you're okay."

"This was a bad time to tell you. I'm sorry. But I'm going to take Nola over next week and talk to the director."

"Okay," Iris says. "We'll talk more tonight, after . . ." She shrugs, smiles. "After whatever this is!"

She gets in her car and starts the engine, checks her face in the rearview mirror. *Whatever this is,* indeed. Meeting John has made her aware that she has been feeling a clanky kind of loneliness, a sorrow that seems to steal in sideways when she least expects it. It makes her feel empty, almost ill, when it comes. This feeling is better.

It is precisely six o'clock when Iris reaches the farmhouse. When she goes down the driveway, she notices that it's not nearly as bumpy as it was; many of the ruts have been filled in. Leaning against a nearby tree is a shovel, a new one, from the looks of it. Has he smoothed out the driveway for her? She thinks he must have, and she feels an uptick of pleasure, even pride.

She pulls up to the end of the drive, nearly even with the house, and waits for a moment, thinking he might come right out. No. She toots the horn. Nothing.

She gets out of the car and goes to the back door, knocks lightly, then more loudly.

Still nothing. She opens the door and steps in. "John?"

He's not in the kitchen. He's added some dishes, she sees, a metal platter featuring a rooster, a dented black teapot. On the kitchen table is the same stack of books she saw before, but there is also a worn black journal and what looks to be a fountain pen. She steps closer.

Yes, a beautiful blue fountain pen, and she picks it up, even though she feels she should not. For Iris, fountain pens have a declarative feel in hand, much as fabric does. She runs her fingers along the smooth, cool surface, lays it in her palm to appreciate the small, compact weight, then sets the pen back down. What she really wants to see is the nib, but what if he walks in and sees her fooling around with his personal things? She would never open his journal, but what temptation lies there! She moves away from the table to the window, looks to see if he might be outside. No.

"John?" she calls again. "*John?*"

No answer, but there is a scrabbling sound in the walls that makes her shudder.

She opens the door to the next room. On top of an old iron bed frame, serving as what Iris guesses is a mattress, are a few flannel shirts placed end to end and stuffed with something. The quilt that he offered her on that rainy day when she last saw him is folded at the bottom. There is a wooden nightstand missing a drawer. On top of the nightstand is another candle, this one a cream-colored pillar, or what is left of it: his bedside lamp, she presumes. What must it be like to read in bed by candlelight, the only sounds the pages turning and the wind blowing and the cicadas singing in the trees? On a chair in the corner she sees some clothes, folded neatly, and a few pairs of shoes lined up beside it.

It occurs to her suddenly that something might have happened to him. He's staying out here alone—illegally, she supposes. Anyone could have come here: a rowdy group of kids, a thief, a wild animal. The cops, too, although the cops in Mason were more like Andy-of-Mayberry police than anything else. They'd probably take him out for a meal and then ask him if he wouldn't mind leaving in the next day or so, if that would be all right. They'd probably offer him a lift to the outskirts of town and make sure the temperature in the squad car was adjusted to his comfort.

He might have gotten ill and gone to the ER.

But surely he would have called her if that had happened.

Called her! Of course! That's what she can do, is call him. She feels foolish for not having thought of that before. But there's something about being here in this old house that makes you forget about things like cellphones. There's something here that makes modern-day trappings feel . . . well, off your back.

She goes to the car for her phone. She'll call him and

there will be a simple explanation for why he's not here. He might be walking back from town right now, carrying his latest find. Iris saw a paint-by-number image of lilac bushes at a garage sale just yesterday that she almost bought for him, thinking he'd appreciate the irony and maybe even the painting itself. Twenty-five cents.

If he is walking home, she'll be able to drive out and meet him and give him a lift back here so that he can drop off his treasures. They'll be a bit late getting back to her house to dinner, but she'll give Maddy a heads-up. Eggplant lasagna only gets better when you let it sit out, anyway.

She finds John's number in her phone's history and calls it. While she waits for him to answer, she looks around again to see if he's out in the yard. Wouldn't it be funny if he came up behind her and startled her again?

He is not behind her. He is not anywhere that she can see. Nor does he answer his phone; she is met with a generic message informing her that the person at this number is not available. Iris goes back in the house and calls out John's name once more. She looks in the two rooms of the house again. She doesn't want to venture farther; she can see that the next room is empty but for some tattered lace curtains, and the stairs to go up are treacherous-looking: missing boards, what looks like rot.

She goes back outside, a dullness in her. A kind of shame. On the way to the car, she breaks off a few branches of the lilacs that are left, even though she's not sure they'll be alive by the time she gets home.

When Iris pulls into her own driveway, Nola runs out, shouting, "You're late! You're late! For a very important date!" She looks around Iris—for John, presumably.

"He's not coming," Iris says, getting out of the car.

Nola holds herself very still. "Why not?"

Iris walks over to sit on the bottom porch step, folds her hands between her knees. It's lovely out, everything covered by a golden wash of early-evening light. "He wasn't there when I came to pick him up. And he didn't answer when I tried calling him."

"How come?"

"Well, I don't know."

Nola scratches her elbow. "Do you feel sad?"

"Do I look sad?"

"Yes, you look like this." Nola hangs her head and turns her mouth down.

"I guess I'm disappointed," Iris says. "But the good thing is, we have a delicious dinner that you and Mommy and I can enjoy."

"It was supposed to be for company," Nola says. "I made a decoration for the table that is paper flowers but in a real vase. They are on pipe cleaners is how they stand up."

"I can't wait to see them. Are you hungry?"

Nola spins around in a circle. "I am staaarrrrving."

"Well, okay, then," Iris says, getting up. "Let's eat!"

Maddy, standing at the top of the stairs, gives Iris a look as she passes by.

Iris shakes her head.

"Not coming?" Maddy says, and Iris calls over her shoulder, "Nope!" How funny to sound so gay.

Well, she wanted to talk to Maddy, anyway. In private. After Nola goes to bed, they'll have privacy. And a lot of leftovers.

An arm hangs from a tree. An arm? No. A branch. The elephant grass they are moving through hisses like snakes. He is not afraid. Fear is walled off in an area of his chest—he feels it like a stone but he is not afraid. It is as though extra eyes and extra ears have grown all over him, as though even his skin were hyperalert. He tries to make no noise whatsoever. A cough is a death sentence.

There are three of them up ahead of the rest of the line, cutting the trail. It's exhausting work; no one can do it for more than half an hour at a time. But it's their turn. Sanchez is first, John is second, Beauregard is third. It's hot, so humid. His breath feels like pudding in his lungs. A shot rings out and Sanchez goes down, hit in the throat. Blood geysers up and Sanchez gurgles and twitches, then goes still. Another shot and Beauregard drops and begins screaming, "My foot! My foot!"

"Medic!" John cries. A bullet flies by his own forehead,

just missing him. He looks back at Sanchez, the flies al-
ready on him, then at Beauregard, crying and shaking and
moaning, "Not here, not here! Ma! Ma! Ma!" John drops
his gun and begins to take off everything on his body. His
helmet, his rucksack, the metal container he carries beneath
it with letters from Laura and from his mother, with paper-
back books and his notebook and pens. He takes off his belt
of extra ammo, his uniform, his underwear, his boots and
his filthy socks, his dog tags. Then he stands there. Because
just get this over. It doesn't get over. The rest of the line
catches up to him and Gaines grabs his arm and says,
"What the fuck, Loney?" The next day John talks to a doctor
and the day after that he is back at it.

Out in the field where he is lying, the birds have roosted
in the cottonwood trees. John makes his hands into fists
and pounds his eyes. *Unsee. Unsee.* He will never not see.
So many years ago, and he still sees. More than fifty-eight
thousand names on the Wall, five of them boys sixteen
years old who lied about their age so that they could enlist.
More than fourteen hundred killed on the last day.

He sits up, then stands and starts making his way back
to the house. Night is coming on.

He is here now. There is a bed, there is a roof, there are
walls.

Before he goes in, he sees a wasps' nest hanging from a

corner of the house. It's a good foot and a half long. If he can make it up the rotted steps inside, he can knock it off through an upstairs window. Although why.

He's almost out of water. He's almost out of food. He's almost out of money.

Things hurt.

He sits at the kitchen table and lights the candle with a hand that is still shaking. Opens a book. Shuts it. Opens his journal and uncaps his pen. Writes nothing.

He moves to the window and watches the stars come out one by one, as though they're just being made and coming off an assembly line. He says her name, just to hear his own voice for the first time today. *Laura.*

He moves to his bed and lifts the quilt to find his phone. Almost entirely out of juice—he didn't make it to anywhere where he could charge it today. There is a message, and he wonders if he should listen—shouldn't he save what little power is left in case he needs it? It's probably just Proud Mary. He owes it to her to let her know once and for all that he'll never return.

He listens to the message, and it's not Mary. It's that lovely woman who came and picked lilacs and then invited him to dinner. Iris. It was for tonight, then. This is Saturday, then.

He looks over at the window: completely dark out now. It's too late to try to walk there. It's too late, period.

He flings himself down on his bed and puts his arm over his eyes. His father: *You were born a loser, and you'll die one. It's a wonder you're my son. Maybe you're not.* His mother: *Ah, Johnny, don't listen. Come here to your mother.*

Eight years old, and he steals her a bottle of Coca-Cola for Mother's Day. "Just what I wanted," she tells him, and she claps her hands. She drinks only a little at a time; it takes her three days to finish it. Then she wraps it in foil and uses it to hold the wildflowers he brings her with the same sense of helpless hope.

Making Her Way
Back Home

"Well, girls, I have nothing to confess," Toots says, yanking on her sweater to stretch it out over her belly. "Can you believe it?" And then, as though someone else has said this, her mouth drops open.

"Maybe you just don't want to tell us your sin," Karen says. "Which is fine. My husband just got back from a retreat and they talked a lot about how it's not always healthy or necessary for people to share wrongdoings with their pastors. 'The silence of the lambs?' I asked him, but he didn't find that funny."

"No, that's not it," Toots says. "I thought all week about what I might want to confess, and I just don't have anything. I haven't done anything wrong. I have nothing to be embarrassed about or to figure out. Nothing."

Gretchen nods enthusiastically. "She told me when she came into my store yesterday, she said, 'I have nothing to confess. What am I going to do?' And I said, 'Are you sure? Seems like we always have *some*thing.' But she said no."

Toots says, "One time, when I was a little girl, I was in line for confession and I didn't really have any sins that time, either. So I just said things like, 'I didn't always pay attention in church.' You know, that caliber of sin. Like, way less than venial. And the priest was real quiet and finally he said, 'Well, you are a *good* girl. You just go in peace now, and God bless you.' I said, 'What about my penance?' and he said, 'You have no penance! You're a *good* girl!' Well, I just strutted out of that booth, let me tell you. But now . . . well, I'm not proud that I don't have anything to confess. 'Cause maybe I forgot something bad that I did. Or, you know, blocked it. What I decided, though, is that I would like to forfeit my time. I'll forfeit it to one of the newbies."

All of the women turn to look at Maddy and Iris, who, seated side by side, look at each other.

"Uh . . . I guess I'm not quite ready," Iris says. "But thanks."

All eyes on Maddy. She swallows, then says, "Okay. I'll go. Just give me a minute. I'll be right back." She leaves the room.

"Anyone need anything while we're waiting?" Rosemary asks. "I'm getting more pie. I almost never eat dessert, but, Lord, this pie is worth every one of its bazillion calories."

Karen, who made the sticky toffee pudding pie, beams. "I make this for funeral lunches," she says. "Even the grief-stricken gobble it up. Good thing I made the large size!"

"I could have another slice," Toots says. And then Gretchen says she'd like another one, and then Joanie and then Dodie.

"For Pete's sake," Rosemary says, "there's only one piece left!" She goes into the kitchen and comes out with the pie plate and many forks. "We'll pass it around," she says.

The women have just about finished the pie when Maddy comes back into the room.

She sits in her chair, clears her throat, and begins speaking.

"What's that?" Dodie says. "You'll need to talk louder, honey; I can't hear a word you're saying."

"Sorry," Maddy says. "I was just saying I don't really know how to begin except to sort of dive in the middle. So. I am lying to my husband, and I have been for some time."

Silence.

Then, "Lying about what?" Toots asks, gently.

Maddy begins to weep. "About why I came here. About who I am. About what I want to do. About how I don't even *know* what I want to do! About how scared I am that he'll want to leave me if I tell him all that I'm feeling. About how *not* telling him how I'm feeling will make him want to leave me, too. I keep . . . withholding, and I can feel it making us grow apart, and I know if I lose him, I'll have lost the best thing I ever had, except for my daughter." She stops crying and wipes the tears from her face. Now her voice lowers to barely audible again. "And also I'm lying because I don't tell him how much I . . . don't like myself."

"What?" Dodie says, leaning forward.

Maddy says nothing, and Karen, seated next to Dodie, tells her, "She said she doesn't like herself."

"Well, for heaven's sake, why would she say that?"

Karen jerks her head in Maddy's direction, and Dodie addresses her directly. "Why would you say that, honey?"

Maddy sighs. "It goes a long way back, I guess. My mother died when I was just a few weeks old. She went to the doctor and my father stayed home with me because I had a cold. She got in a car accident, and I don't think my father could ever let go of blaming me."

"But you were an infant!" says Rosemary. "You weren't responsible for anything!"

"I know it doesn't make sense," Maddy says. "But I think it's true that he blamed me. We never got along, my father and I. He never shared very much about my mother unless I asked him directly, and for the most part, I didn't know what to ask. 'Did she like the color red?' I mean, what could I ask? I would find something. . . . 'Was this hers?' 'Yes,' he'd say, and take it from me. And that was all. He never . . . Well, let's just say it was a very lonely time, growing up. I tried not to let things in. I tried not to care. I tried to become hard, but . . . Anyway, I guess I could go on for a long time about what happened to me growing up, but what matters is what I am now. And what I am now . . ."

Maddy leans forward, her hands clasped upon the table. "I guess I feel I can't love properly. Except for my daughter. Anyone else, things get in the way. I guess *I* get in the way. If someone tells me something nice, I might thank them, but inside it's as though I'm holding my hand up like a traffic cop: *Stop.*

"If someone hugs me, I don't hug back so much as wait for it to be over. For me, love hurts. Even when it's good, it hurts. Even when I recognize the fact that I want love, and, like everyone else, need it, I fear it. And I don't have any idea how to tell my husband that what's keeping me from him is not my lack of love for him but for myself."

"Why don't you just say it like that?" Toots asks.

"I *can't.* I don't want him to know that I . . . I don't want him to know."

"You know what I think?" Gretchen says. "I think love is all about risk. And reinvention. And honesty and revelation. And if you don't have that in a relationship, you don't grow, and you don't stay true to what you started together."

"I think it's more than that," Karen says. "Maddy, I know what it's like to despise yourself. I had a lot of years of therapy to try to overcome feelings like that."

"*You?*" asks Joanie.

"Yes, me. I did everything from intensive talk therapy every week for five years to looking at myself in the mirror every day and saying, 'I love you.' It took the longest time for me to feel as though I meant it. It seemed a ridiculous exercise to me, saying those words to myself. I would say 'I love you,' but I would be thinking the opposite. I remember having a dream in those days that I was sitting in a circle of people who were nominally my friends. And one by one they were saying things they hated about me. And when it came to me, I said, 'You forgot about . . . ' and I listed other faults that I had."

Joanie's face is full of concern. "You never told any of this to us!"

Karen shrugs. "It was a long time ago. I'm past it. I don't want to invite any of it back into my life. Except when it comes to trying to help someone else who's suffering from the same kind of thing I dealt with for so long."

"Why don't you try the mirror thing, Maddy?" Joanie asks.

"I don't know that it would help me very much," Maddy says. "I feel like you need to be able to hear that someone else loves you."

Karen holds up a finger. "Except. What I learned is that you've got to start with you. It's wonderful to hear someone say they love you. But unless you love yourself, the words won't stick. Do you know what I mean?"

Maddy shrugs.

"Something else that helped me," Karen says, "is a photo my best friend sent me when I was really going through it. It was something she photoshopped. She put together a picture of me as a two-year-old, sitting on Santa's lap, and myself as an adult. On my child self's face is a look of such longing. Such longing and such fear. I won't touch Santa, I'm afraid to, but you can see how much I want to. I've got my hands raised, but I'm keeping my arms by my side; I can't move forward. In the place of Santa, my friend put in a photo of myself as an adult, and I've got my hands on my child self's shoulders, and on my adult face is a little humor, a lot of love, and it's as though I'm saying, 'You're going to be all right.' And I am all right now. I believe you will be too, Maddy."

"I can't do therapy," Maddy says. "I can't go more into that darkness."

"The only way to get out of that darkness is to go into it," Karen says. "That's how you can come out the other side. You're going to have to hurt more before you finally feel better."

"I guess," Maddy says.

Beneath the table, Iris briefly touches Maddy's knee.

"I just want to say one more thing," Karen says. "And that is, don't rely on your child to save you. That's too much of a burden to put on her."

"I'm not relying on Nola to save me!" Maddy says, but even as she says it, she realizes she may be doing that very thing.

The room goes quiet, and finally Toots says, "Maddy, this might not be the place for your problem to be solved. But it is the place where you can talk about it. I think I speak for all of us when I say that although we may not know you well, we care for you a lot. And we respect your courage in saying what you just did."

"Thank you," Maddy says. "And . . . well, I guess I've said enough for one night, if that's okay."

"That's just fine," Toots says. "Will you come back next week, when someone else is in the hot seat?"

Maddy picks up the nearly empty pie tin and scrapes her fork across the very last remains. "Yes." And then, smiling, "Of course."

Toots looks at her watch. "We have some time, if anyone has anything else. . . ."

"Well," Dodie says, "I don't know how much of a confession this is, but I've never told anyone this. Sometimes I hold on to my belly and rock it like it's a baby."

"*Why?*" Joanie asks.

"It's comforting," Dodie says. "You should try it."

"Holding your belly?"

"No! Your own!"

Joanie puts her hands around her middle and moves them slightly side to side. "You're right," she says. "They should teach this in yoga classes."

Mea Culpa

❈

On a Sunday morning, Nola is in her pajamas, just out of bed, and is looking out the kitchen window while Iris pores over recipes for her adult class coming up in a few days: Just Peachy. She wants a crisp or a crumble that uses peaches and ginger, although she's also attracted to a peach pie that uses dulce de leche. Maddy has gone out to breakfast with her father in one last attempt to connect with him.

"This is the funniest rain," Nola says. "It's not like regular rain, it's coming down in clumps."

Iris looks up, and the child is right: the rain is like one of the options on her showerhead, a kind of pulsing, gloppy rain.

"It looks like it's trying to learn how to rain," Nola says. And then, "Can we go out in it?"

"Out in the rain?"

She nods.

Iris thinks about this. Why not? It's warm again today; there are inviting puddles to splash in.

"Would your mom be okay with that?"

Nola says nothing at first. But then, "You are the mom now," she says.

Iris crosses her arms and stares. Nola stares back.

"Oh, all right," Iris says. "We'll go out together, for just a little while. But let's eat breakfast first. What would you like?"

"Something fast."

"Granola and strawberries?"

"Strawberries and yogurt?" Nola asks. "Granola takes too long to chew."

Iris prepares it for them both. She envies Nola for the way she is always in a rush to do everything, the way she rises so quickly to the possibility of joy. Most of all, she envies Nola her default setting of goodwill toward man, beast, or weather.

Iris gathers up towels and puts them on the porch for when they come in. Then, hand in hand, they go out in the street and begin splashing in the puddles. After a few minutes, Link comes out of his house in his swimming trunks, and Iris thinks she should go in and leave the children to play—though Link would object to being called a child, rather than the preteen that he is. Iris has grown awfully fond of Link, and he's wonderful with Nola. He's taught her about surface tension, about air pressure, about the number of muscles and bones in the human body. He's shown her blood cells and salt crystals under his microscope, explained to her why people breathe, what a balance beam does for tightrope walkers. They watch You-Tube animal videos together. Maddy is strict about the amount of time Nola is allowed to spend looking at screens, but she cuts her daughter some slack when it comes to watching things like puppies learning to walk down the stairs.

Iris walks up to the porch screen door and is just about to open it when she hears a voice calling her name. She turns around and sees John standing there, drenched. Over his jeans he's wearing a white shirt, a worn sport coat that's a bit short in the sleeves for him, and a wide, striped tie that looks about as natural on him as earrings on a crow.

She says nothing, and he walks over to her, smiles. "Are we destined to meet only in rain, then, do you think?"

She doesn't smile.

"I came to apologize, Iris. I'm ashamed to tell you this, but I forgot it was Saturday. I didn't know it was Saturday. I've since made myself a calendar, though, and I am happy to tell you that I know that today is Tuesday. And I found a day job clearing out a basement today, and I made a fair amount of money for my trouble, so now I can ask you to have dinner with me. On me."

Nola hollers from the street, where she has been splashing in the gutters, "Who is that?"

He turns to her. "I'm John. That's my name, John Loney."

Nola brushes wet hair from her eyes. "You were supposed to come here and eat, but you didn't come. We had eggplant lasagna, and I made cupcakes for you."

"Ah, me. I'm sorry. Mea culpa."

"What?"

"I said, 'Mea culpa.' Means my fault. But here's what I'm wondering. Don't you think you need a boat to float in all that water? Maybe a raft?"

"I have a bunch of Popsicle sticks," Link says. "And some twine."

"That will do," John says, and starts walking toward the children.

"Hello?" Iris says.

He turns around.

"Did you mean dinner tonight?"

"Yes. If you're willing."

"All right," Iris says. The words fall out of her mouth before she has quite made her decision. This is the way things seem to go with this man. To Nola, she says, "Only a few more minutes out there, all right?"

Back in the house, Iris stands at the window and dries herself and her hair off. She mutters, "Idiot!" meaning herself. But she doesn't feel like an idiot. She feels like Nola, face-to-face with an opportunity for joy. Why not take it? Why not?

She sees John kneel in the grass to help the children

finish constructing the raft. Then the three of them stand together watching as it sails off, spinning and spinning in the current. Nola and Link laugh and splash and look up at the sky with their heads back and their mouths open and their arms held out. As for John, he seems impervious to both the rain and the successful launch. He stands unmoving, with his hands in his pockets. It unnerves her, in a way, but it also widens a stubborn V in her heart. She shivers, then grows warm. In a little while, she'll invite him in.

Maddy leaves The Chicken or the Egg, the restaurant where she just had breakfast with her father. She feels that trying to talk to him was awful, nearly useless. And yet they made plans for breakfast next month, should she still be here then. She told him she was thinking about moving her family back to Mason, and her father nodded. And that was all. Didn't say, "That would be nice." Didn't say, "I hope you do," or, "Maybe that's not such a good idea." Didn't say anything. He smiled and then looked at his watch. And then Maddy said, "Well, I'll let you know." And her father said, "Good." He cleared his throat and said it again: "Good." When they parted, he patted her back in a way that had her suddenly tear up, though she was careful not to let him see.

She isn't ready to get in the car and go home. She decides to walk a little. She's gone a few blocks when she sees a familiar figure coming toward her. Is it . . . ? It is. Nola's father, the man who abandoned her years ago. She hasn't seen him since before Nola was born. He's older, of course, but otherwise unchanged, still well built, still awfully good-looking. She stands still for a second, then keeps walking. He nods when he gets to her, starts to go past, then stops. "*Maddy?*"

"Hello, Anderson."

"Wow. Haven't seen you for a while!"

"About eight years."

He rubs the top of his head. "That right?" He's wearing a wedding ring.

"Yes, that's right."

"I heard you were living in New York City."

"Right."

"Huh. I'm moving, too, but not there. Wouldn't live there for a million bucks."

"Yes, well, it's not for everyone."

"I'm going to Florida. Me and the wife. She got some fancy job there, so . . . we got two more days here and that's it."

"I hope you'll be happy there."

"Leastwise it will be warm in the winter. You know?"

"Uh-huh."

"So . . . you kept the kid, right?"

She laughs. "Yeah. I kept the kid."

He nods. "Okay, well . . ."

She smiles. "Goodbye, Anderson."

"Maddy. Listen, I'm sorry I . . . Well, I'm sorry."

"It worked out all right. Good luck to you." Funny. She means it.

She walks on and begins to feel a lifting inside, a hope that maybe all she needs to do is ask Matthew, and he will agree to move back. They will move back, she will begin a kind of work on herself in earnest, and everything will get better and better. She turns around to go and get her car. She'll call Matthew, then drive home.

He answers the phone with a curt "Yeah."

". . . Matthew?"

"Yeah!"

"Well, *hi*! How are you?"

"All right. You?"

"I just had breakfast with my dad. That went about as well as you might think."

"Uh-huh."

"What about you? What have you been doing?"

"Nothing much. Went to Roberto's for pizza last night with Nick and Betsy. Then I went to Brooklyn Bowl for a concert. It was great. I met some people there, and afterward we went to a bar that just opened and got a drink called Erupting Volcano. Very cool drink. How's Nola?"

"She's great. She misses you."

"I miss her, too."

"Matthew? I—"

"Listen, Maddy, I'm sorry, but I've got to go down to the laundry room and get my clothes out of the dryer. You know how everybody gets all pissed off if you hog the dryer."

"Oh, yeah, of course! We can talk later."

"I'll call you tomorrow sometime. Kiss Nola."

He hangs up.

I met some people there. . . . Who did he meet?

Maddy rests her head on the steering wheel, then starts the car.

When Maddy opens the front door, she sees her daughter from the hallway. She's in the kitchen, standing on a chair stationed before Lucille's venerable old KitchenAid mixer, adding chocolate chips to whatever she's making. Nola sees her, and, over the noise of the mixer, shouts, "These are cookies you don't even have to bake! And they are chocolate-chip and peanut butter and oatmeal all together!"

"Wow," Maddy says. She comes into the kitchen and stops in her tracks. Link is sitting at the kitchen table, poring over a book of experiments, and opposite him is a stranger, a man dressed in Iris's beautiful lavender silk robe, drinking coffee.

"Oh. Hey," Maddy says.

"Hi, Maddy," says Link, not looking up from his book.

The man rises. Then, looking down at the robe, "Oh. I got drenched in the rain. My clothes are in the dryer."

"I see," Maddy says, though she does not. "I'll be right back," she says, but she has no intention of coming right back. She wants to go to her bedroom and be alone.

But as soon as she's closed the bedroom door and moved to sit at the edge of the bed, she hears a light knock at the door, the uneven rapping that Nola does.

"Come in!" Maddy says, trying to make her voice happy and bright.

But there's no fooling Nola. The child is wise beyond her years; she always has been.

"What's wrong?" she asks her mother.

Maddy smiles.

"Are you sad?" she asks.

"I guess I am, a little."

"Why?"

Oh, what to say. That she's worried she's lost her marriage? That being with her father for barely an hour seems to have dismantled the frail scaffolding of self-confidence she worked so hard to build? That she doesn't know where she belongs, both in the specific and in the general senses of the word?

Don't rely on your child to save you.

"You know what, honey? It's just a weird sort of mood. Like a cloud in the sky. Do you ever have that happen?"

Nola plays with the doorknob and considers this. "I

guess so. But when it happens, I just go do something else."

"That's very smart. I'll be down in just a minute. I'm dying to taste those cookies!"

"I'll put them on your favorite plate."

"Good."

Nola starts to skip out, then turns around. "Wait. Is it the one with the little violets?"

"Nope. The one with the little roses."

"Oh, yeah. Okay, see you down there!"

Nola clatters down the stairs and Maddy sighs, clasps her hands together, and hangs her head. When she was pregnant with Nola and living here with Arthur and Lucille, Arthur once came upon her curled up in a corner of her room, lost in misery the way she is now. "Mind if I sit here?" he asked, indicating the bed where she had cocooned herself in a quilt. She shrugged, which was as much of a yes as she could offer in those days. She was friendless, abandoned by both her father and her horrible boyfriend, and she was pregnant with a child she was determined to keep, even though she was scared to death about the idea.

"Lucille's making fish for supper," Arthur told her. He wrinkled his nose, which seemed to make his ears stick out more. He was wearing a white shirt that day, blue old-man pants, cinched high at the waist and shiny from over-ironing, and red suspenders. His thin hair stood up in the back from having taken his beloved hat off; Arthur was a man who believed a gentleman didn't wear a hat in the house. "She made me go and buy *fish*."

Maddy said nothing.

"You like fish?" he asked.

"Not really," she answered.

"Me, neither," said Arthur. "Fish*ing* I like, 'long as I don't catch anything. Oh, it's wonderful to fish. All the sounds the water makes, why, it's like a language. That long green and yellow grass swaying underwater like a hula dance, the way the boat rocks just a little bit, like it's saying, 'There now, there now.' I guess we all of us like to be soothed, no matter how old we are—isn't that so?"

Again, Maddy said nothing.

"I go out in the boat with my fishing rod, but I don't put any bait on it."

"Why do you even go fishing if you don't want to catch fish?" Maddy asked. Her tone was crueler than she meant it to be.

"Well, that's a fair question and here's the answer. I like the peace that comes with fishing. If I went out and just lay on the riverbank, I'd feel guilty, thinking of what else I should be doing. All the things that needed doing. But with my fishing pole, everybody thinks I *am* doing something!"

"Why does everybody care so much about what other people think?" Maddy asked, and the bitterness in her voice was plain.

"Another good question that I've thought about myself.

To tell you the truth, I think it's a design flaw. There are quite a few design flaws in us humans, you know. More than in animals and plants. And I guess we have to cope with them. Don't have to like them, just have to cope with them."

From downstairs came the voice of Lucille yelling up at them. "Do I have to spell it out? It's D-I-N-N-E-R-T-I-M-E!" Maddy knew just how she'd look: flush-faced, her hand gripping the knob on the stair rail, a dishtowel tucked into her waist, one sneakered foot on the tread to help her lean in and holler better.

Arthur leaned forward. "Coming!" he shouted, and his voice cracked like a teenager's. And then to Maddy: "We gotta go. She says your baby needs fish because it's brain food and by God she's going to feed you fish. So here's what you do. She's making catfish in cornmeal batter and the batter is real good. So when you take a bite of fish, you tell your brain, 'My, this batter is good,' and then you quick eat some mashed potatoes, and you know nobody makes better mashed potatoes than Lucille. And then quick eat another bite of fish and then some green beans—they're good, too. Like that. Alternate. Am I right? You're going to have the bad but you sure enough are going to have the good, too. You just concentrate on that cornmeal batter."

He pulled a small gift wrapped in yellow paper from his pocket. "I got this for the baby today, at a garage sale. Ten cents."

"What is it?" Maddy asked.

"*Do I have to come up there and drag you two down?*" they heard.

"Open it quick," Arthur said, "and then come down before she has a stroke." He looked at her and smiled. "Listen to me. You know what? You're the top."

"The top of what?"

"Oh, my. Cole Porter?"

She looked blankly at him.

"We'll have some fun later," Arthur said. "I'll play you a record you'll love!" With one finger wagging in the air, he sang, "*You're the top! / You're Mahatma Gandhi!*"

He went out into the hall. "Sure smells good!" he called down to Lucille.

Maddy opened the package. A tiny book about fish. And weren't they beautiful. Their round, clear eyes, their fan-dance tails, the rainbow colors of their shiny scales. They were beautiful.

Now Maddy closes her eyes for the briefest second. A sealing-in of memory, a benediction, a wish that she could once again be under Arthur's care. "Truluv," she called him. He was that. True love. She is so happy to be staying in his room. It's almost as though he's still taking care of her.

But now she is a mother and responsible for someone else's care. And here before her is Miss Cornmeal Batter herself; Nola has come up to get her.

"Didn't you hear me calling you?"

Maddy pats her lap. "Come here."

Nola climbs onto her lap and Maddy pushes the girl's hair behind her ears and says, "I was just up here thinking about you."

"You were?"

"Yup."

The girl's voice grows small. "And it made you sad?"

"Oh, no!" Maddy says, laughing. "You make me happy! I was just thinking of how you are growing and changing, and you know what? I wish I could be just like you."

"You do?"

"Yes. I just love you so much."

"I love you, too."

"Nola, who is that man down there wearing Iris's robe?"

"Oh, that's John. He's the man who didn't come to dinner. He's fun! He helped us build a raft to sail in the gutter. And he's taking Iris out for dinner tonight. She told me. After his clothes get all dry, they're going to buy some seed and then they're going to plant stuff and then they're going out to dinner. They invited me to help plant, but I'm going to help Link. I'm his assistant. Like a magician's assistant, only I am a science assistant."

"Where are they planting the seeds?" She hopes it's not in Arthur's garden. She wants Arthur's garden to stay the same.

Nola offers an elaborate shrug and hops off her mother's lap. "I don't know. I think in his garden. But you should come down, because your cookies are ready and also, guess what Link is going to show us? How to make invisible ink. And how to make a cloud in a jar."

"You're kidding!"

"See?" Nola says. "Better come and be with us, now."

Maddy rises gratefully up to follow her daughter downstairs. You can't ask your children to save you. But they do it anyway.

Closer

John leans over Iris to touch the tiny pearls scattered over her T-shirt. "Are these from Tahiti? Is this cotton from Egypt? Because that's what you deserve, Iris."

She laughs.

He doesn't. He flops down onto his back and puts an arm over his eyes. "I can feel my hands and I can feel my feet. I can feel that I am here. I mean, all of me, inside and out. This is unusual." He looks over at her, one eye closed. "Maybe that makes no sense."

"No, it's . . . It makes sense. I know what you mean."

"Do you?"

"Yes. I think so."

"Well, then."

He looks away again, closes his eyes.

They are lying out in a field near the barn, where they planted seeds for what will be an impressive vegetable garden, should things take. There will be four kinds of lettuce, zucchini, tomatoes, onions, peas, beets, corn, basil, carrots, potatoes, watermelon, rhubarb. Iris has never planted a vegetable garden before, didn't know anything about preparing or amending the soil, didn't know how far down to dig for the seeds, didn't know about making the little hills to plant the zucchini in, didn't know how good it was to plant after a rain, didn't know anything, really. But she was eager to learn. She helped in every way, and her body is feeling it now. But it's good pain, the virtuous kind she used to feel after she went to the gym in Boston. This work is better than being in a gym. The sun on your back, the smell of earth on your hands, the birds lining up on tree branches to supervise, the clouds making for a bit of shade, then moving on, the little sounds of industry created by digging and patting, by watering from cleaned-out tin cans. She wonders how John will sustain this garden without water on the land, but if the season stays as rainy as it has been, he has a good chance of getting things going.

"I want to tell you something, Iris."

"Tell me."

"It's not a pleasant thing."

"That's okay." Now she's a little nervous. Still, "You can tell me anything," she says, and it has happened again, words falling from her mouth without any forethought.

"I want to tell you why I'm homeless. If I can. I want to try."

She gets up on one elbow to look down at him, his eyes still closed. The shape of his lips makes her feel as though she's gone liquid. He has such a noble profile: such a fine forehead, such a straight nose, such beautiful cheekbones. She looks at the beat of his heart in his neck, at the rise of muscles on his chest, down his arms, in his long legs. Dirt is caked in the lines of his hands. She spies a little cut on his palm, untended, and a sense of tenderness all out of proportion to the wound yanks at her stomach. She wants to put her head on his shoulder and feel their arms wrapped around each other, offering that timeless and intimate shelter. She wants to lie very still beside him for hours, while the sounds of the natural world go on about them. Also, she wants to take off her clothes and admit him. Instead, she lies back down and closes her own eyes, to listen.

He speaks in a curious monotone, as though to add inflection would make the telling too hard. "A few days after my wife left me, I was lying in my bed one night and I had to take a piss. And I didn't care that I had to take a piss. I didn't care about anything. I just lay there and eventually it was like my bladder burst, and I wet the bed. Then I got up. I got up, and I got my rifle and I crawled out the window and onto the roof and began to shoot. I shot at the stars. I shot at the trees. Someone called the cops and they came and arrested me and took me down to the station and locked me up. They put me in a cell with some other guys who were all a mess like me. And nobody asked any questions of me. Not one person cared that I'd pissed myself, and was reeking. Not one person cared anything about me. And it was the first time since I'd come back from 'Nam that I felt I could relax. It was the first time I didn't feel the world closing in on me, that . . . *pressure*. I thought, 'I don't care about anything anymore and I don't want to. I don't care about anyone and I don't want anyone to care about me. I can't carry it. I can't *carry* it.' After they let me out, I never went home. I hit the streets. Every now and then, I'd try living inside, with other people. Be a roommate. Be a lover. But it never worked for long. I needed to be out. Free. These days, I only . . . Well, I wake up each morning and wait for the sun to break the sky. And when it doesn't, I get up."

He looks over at her. "I know I'm not right. I won't ever be right again. There are days when I feel held together by cobwebs. But then there are other days. Like this one."

Iris thinks of Maddy at the last Confession Club. She thinks of the admission that Karen Lundgren made about her own difficulties. All around are broken people, doing the best they can. And getting better. She has faith that John can, too. But she has a question she wants to ask. It is not her business, really. Yet it is, because of the gentle entanglement they have begun. Seeds in the ground. She clears her throat, then speaks quietly. "Why did your wife leave you?"

For a long time, he says nothing. Then, "That's another story." He stands and looks up at the sky. "It'll be dark soon. Let's go into the house now and not talk anymore. Will you come into the house with me, Iris? And after, we'll go to dinner?"

She knows what he's asking. And she rises to her feet and takes his hand.

A lot of people would have something to say about this, Iris and her homeless man. Here's what she has to say about this: *Good.*

Iris is about halfway home from being with John when her confidence fades. She turns off the radio and begins a self-administered interrogation: *What are you doing? This man is clearly unstable! What are you doing? Yes, a million people have doubts and insecurities, questions of self-worth, but a man who shoots a rifle from the roof?*

When she pulls into the driveway, she sees the dim figure of Maddy sitting on the porch steps, holding a glass of wine. She sits down beside her. "Hey," she says, wearily.

"Well, *hey*," Maddy says, and if her voice were a dog it would have its ears perked up. "Want a glass of wine?"

Iris nods. While Maddy goes into the house to fetch it, Iris thinks about whether to tell Maddy what has happened. No. Not yet.

Maddy comes out onto the porch again, and the screen door bangs behind her. "Shhhh!" she tells it. She sits beside Iris, gives her a glass, and holds up her own to clink. The women take a sip and then Maddy says, "You slept with him, didn't you?"

"Oh, God," Iris says, and drops her head.

"No judgment here," Maddy says. "He looks like the Marlboro man."

Iris looks at her and frowns. "How do you know about the Marlboro man?"

"I lived with old folks, remember?"

Iris guesses that to Maddy, she's old folks, too.

"What did *you* do tonight?" Iris asks.

"Well. It was a very exciting evening around here. First I watched a candle lift water, courtesy of Link. He explained very clearly to Nola and me why it happened, and you know what? I still don't get it. He put some water on a saucer. Then he put a soda bottle over a lit candle that had been anchored there. When the flame went out, the water rose. Can you think why?"

"Don't look at me," Iris says.

"He also used the static electricity of a comb to bend a stream of water."

"*Okay . . .*"

"You know what?" Maddy says. "I'm a little worried about him. It's too much, these experiments all the time. It's as though he's looking for something not for fun, but for . . . I don't know. It makes me uneasy."

"What does Nola think about the experiments?"

Maddy laughs. "Oh, well, *she's* thrilled! She can't get enough of these experiments. I suppose next she'll be asking me for a lab coat with her name stitched over the pocket."

"We should make her one," Iris says.

"You want to?"

"Sure."

"Can you sew?"

"No. Can you?"

"Nope."

Iris shrugs. "How hard can it be? We've got Lucille's old sewing machine and I'll bet she kept the instruction manual. She loved her instruction manuals."

"That's true."

The women fall silent, and then Maddy says, "So I talked to Matthew today."

"And?"

"I think he's just about had enough."

"Did you ask him about moving back here?"

"It has to be the right time. It'll be a long conversation. Believe me, he wasn't in the right frame of mind. He was angry."

"He misses you," Iris says.

"He misses Nola."

"And *you.*"

Maddy turns to her. "I don't know what to do. This is where I want to be. We don't even lock the door here."

"We should, though," says Iris.

"We should."

"We have Nola to think about."

"Yes. I think about her all the time. In the beginning,

when she was so little, it was easy. It's getting harder now, to try to do a good job with her. I so want to do a good job with her.

"I'm not happy in New York, Iris. You come out your door there and you're in a sea of people you don't know. I guess I never realized until I left how much I depend on familiarity. A lot of people talk about how oppressive small towns are, but for me, they're freeing. And I don't know if New York is the right place for Nola, either. Here, she can go outside in the backyard to play, she has a friend. . . . Oh, I know he's too old for her, but when she starts at the School House, she'll make—"

"So she definitely is going?"

Maddy nods. "I paid the registration fee for both summer sessions today. You know what Nola said when I told her she'd be going to school soon? She said, 'But I have to help Link. How can I do both things? I'll be at my whiz end!'"

Iris laughs, then grows serious. "Maddy, I wonder if you just told Matthew—"

"Right now," Maddy says, "I want to talk about you. I want to know if John was as good as he looks."

"Better," Iris says.

"He's Irish, right?"

"Right."

"Good on you both," Maddy says. Then, standing, "I'm beat. I'm going in. You coming?"

"I'll stay out for just a bit more," Iris says.

Through the screen door, she hears Maddy rinse out her glass in the kitchen, hears her ascend the stairs. She knows Maddy will tiptoe in and stare at Nola sleeping, as she does every night before she goes to bed. Iris does it sometimes, too. She didn't get a child of her own, no, but what a gift to have one living here now. She hopes when Maddy finally gets around to asking Matthew if he'll move back, he'll agree. If he doesn't . . .

She finishes the last of the wine in her glass and thinks of John's parting words to her tonight. They made love, they went to dinner at a small restaurant he'd found the next town over, Hidey's Hole, the best brisket Iris ever tasted. Then they came back to the farm and they lay again on his bed made of hay. As he watched her dress to leave, John said, "Your back reminds me of a swan." He sighed. "Oh, Iris. Bad news. Bad news. I think I am in love with you."

She walked over to him and sat down. "Bad news indeed."

"A veritable disaster," he said.

"Nothing could be worse," she said. "What will we do?"

He studied her face, ran his fingers so lightly up her arm she shivered. "We'll see," he said.

Rules of the Club

❧

"Well, I haven't had macaroni salad like that for years," Toots says. "So much mayonnaise! I forgot how good real mayonnaise is."

Confession Club is at Rosemary's house tonight, and she chose the theme of a picnic dinner: cold fried chicken, macaroni salad, pickled beets, three-bean salad, and a coconut cake with lemon curd filling. She has *Bird Calls of the Great Midwest* on her CD player. At the center of the table, a beautiful vintage wicker hamper is filled with flowers, and Rosemary even scattered some plastic ants—quite realistic-looking!—on the red-and-white-checkered tablecloth.

"Ew!" Gretchen said, when she first saw the ants. She stopped short, causing Dodie, who was following closely behind her, to spill some of the contents of her plate. Luckily it was just a drumstick.

"I'll clean that up," Rosemary said at the same time that Dodie said, "Oh, shit. I'll get that. Damn it!"

"I'll clean the rug," Rosemary said. "You put two dollars in the jar, Dodie."

Joanie claps her hands. "Great! We should have enough for the library to buy another book. We need to amp up our swearing; they want to buy some art books."

Now they have finished their dinner and moved on to a rosé that Rosemary says the clerk at County Line liquors couldn't stop raving about. "He said it had fine *character*," she says. "As if he were providing a job reference! 'Perfect maceration,' he said, which, what does that even mean? And then he said"—and here she makes her voice nasal and superior—"'The taste is an off-dry strawberry, with notes of vanilla and . . . ' Wait. It was so odd. Oh, I remember! 'Forest floor.' Forest *floor*—can you imagine?"

"It is awfully good," Toots says. "But what really tastes good is that extra load of mayonnaise you put in the macaroni salad."

"It wasn't so *much* mayonnaise as it was *real* mayonnaise," Rosemary says. "None of that light mayo for me anymore, it tastes like . . . Well, it tastes like *nothing*."

"Amen," says Toots. "Every time I eat it I try to convince myself that it's more or less the same thing, but it's not. Something really important is missing. I eat a turkey sandwich with that light mayonnaise and I just stare out the window afterward."

"Exactly," says Rosemary. "I've had it with the light stuff. I'm back to real across the board."

"Me, too," says Dodie. "Plus you should start smoking again."

"Why?" Rosemary asks.

Dodie shrugs. "Probably be dead before it killed you this time. At our age, we get a new lease on bad habits."

"Can I get the recipe for that macaroni salad?" Joanie asks.

"Sure," Rosemary says. "It's my mother's. I don't make it often, because whenever I see her writing on the little card—you know how they used to have those cute little index cards with pictures of potholders and such? Such jaunty little potholders on her recipe cards, as if they couldn't be more pleased with themselves for being potholders. And 'From the kitchen of' in such pretty script. But every time I pull out one of her recipe cards, I feel guilty for how mean I was to her."

"We're all mean to our mothers," Gretchen says. "It's a daughter's duty."

"No it isn't," says Rosemary.

"Well, we all do it," Gretchen says. "I don't know why we do it, but we do."

"We have to separate," says Joanie. "We have to push our mothers away so we can be our authentic selves. We have to be mean."

"For all of our lives?" Rosemary says.

"You did it all your *life*?" Karen asks.

"I don't want to talk about it," Rosemary says. "I'm not the one confessing tonight. Who is?"

Gretchen holds up her hand.

"Okay, go," Rosemary says.

Gretchen clears her throat. "Okay. So, this is . . . Well, before my confession, I think I want to say something I'm ashamed of first. Which is that a couple of times a week I go into my closet and cry."

No one says anything.

"It's so Jerry won't hear me," Gretchen says.

"Why shouldn't he hear you?" asks Joanie. "Why don't you tell him what's wrong?"

"Well, that's the confession part. It's about my sons. Who are his sons, too, of course. But the confession is that I wish I could . . . well, I wish I could divorce my sons. Both of them. You talk about mean daughters. But sons can give it out just as bad as any daughter. Last Christmas one of the gifts from my older son was deodorant. Deodorant! A three-pack—that's what was special about it; it was meant to be this great convenience. My other gift from him was an orange mohair sweater so heinous the cat ran away when he saw it. And: I hate to sound like a cliché, but they never call. I always have to be the one to check in. I check in, and do you think at any point they say, 'And how are *you*, Mom?' No. And when I invite them and their snippy wives over to dinner, maybe twice a year, they act like I'm asking them to donate an organ. They will never fill in for me at the store when I have an emergency. No. I have to pay someone overtime because they can't be bothered to pitch in to a business that will someday be

theirs. And their children! Such darling babies and tod-
dlers, but now they positively ransack my house. Nothing
off limits! Their parents sit there doing absolutely nothing
when they go into my desk drawers. And when the children break things, not a word then, either; they don't want
to *shame* them. What's wrong with a little shame? What's
wrong with a little responsibility?

"I don't understand it. It's not how I raised them. I
raised them to be polite, to be empathic, to give to others,
to take responsibility. And I'll tell you, I have had enough.
I don't care if I see them anymore. I don't want to see
them anymore! I don't! Oh, it's a terrible thing to say, I
know. It's a terrible thing to feel! But I just . . . well, I
would rather just get my fill of children—I do love children, you know—I would rather get my fill of children by
babysitting for someone else or volunteering at a daycare
center or something. I mean it. I want to divorce my children."

"Divorce them, then," Dodie says.

Gretchen rolls her eyes. "Right."

"I mean it," Dodie says. "Divorce them, but don't tell
them. I did that with Ralph, may he continue to rest in
peace and be there waiting for me with a big fat gin and
tonic when I join him. I divorced Ralph for an entire year,
and he didn't know a thing about it. For him, nothing
really changed. But for me! Why, I felt like I'd won a trip
to Paris. I felt so carefree! He'd do one of his rude or an-
noying things and it would just roll off me. 'What a jerk,'

I'd think, in a kind of removed way. 'I sure am glad I divorced him.'

"You see, once I did that, got my psychic divorce, I didn't have to take *on* anything of his. In my mind, we weren't a couple any longer. He had his ways, I had mine. Oh, we did things together, still. And I was glad he was there on those stormy nights when the thunder booms so loud it scares the bejesus—"

"Whoops! jar!" Joanie says, and Dodie sighs and looks over at her.

"We don't count 'bejesus.' We talked about that not too long ago, remember? We don't count 'bejesus' or 'crap.'"

Joanie only sips her wine, and Dodie continues.

"Anyway, those times you get scared in the night or you need a jar opened or the car backed out of the garage, well, you have the convenience of having your husband around even if he secretly isn't your husband anymore. Let me tell you, girls, there's nothing like divorcing your husband to make you get along with him." She sits back in her chair, crosses her arms. "So, Gretchen, listen to me. Divorce your children in your mind, and then just go about living your life. Forget about them, and just see how quickly they sense you're not there for them. They'll be all over you in no time. And you know what? When they come back the first time and ask you to do something for them, you say no. Say no! You *always* say yes to those boys, no matter what they ask. Why, I remember when you had tickets to see *Oklahoma!* at the playhouse four months in advance and the day of the play one of your sons asked you to babysit and what did you do? Skipped the play!"

"I know," Gretchen says. "And I love Ado Annie so much. That's the role I wanted when we did the play in high school—remember, Joanie? I wanted it way more than Laurey."

"They had to make you Laurey because you were the prettiest," Joanie says.

"I know," Gretchen says, and sighs. She pushes back the sides of her long red hair.

Dodie coughs, then says in a high, pinched voice, "You didn't even ask your kids if they could reschedule!" She coughs again, clears her throat. "Excuse me. But remember, Gretchen? You didn't even ask them."

"I didn't. You're right."

Dodie shakes her head. "I swear, sometimes I think you're afraid of your kids."

"I am!"

"Oh, my," Toots says. "Let's all bond together over this one. Let's be united in strength and tell Gretchen she can divorce her children. No contact until they call her! Agreed?"

Iris says, "Well, I think Gretchen is the one who has to make the decision."

"I *will* make it!" Gretchen says, and all the women join hands.

Gretchen straightens in her chair. Closes her eyes. "Okay," she says. "I'm doing it. Right here, right now, I divorce my children." She sits back in her chair, a bit stunned-looking, then smiles. "My goodness! I feel better already. It's like someone undid a buckle in my chest." Then she looks a bit worried. "But no one can ever tell anyone I did such a thing."

"Rules of the club," Toots says. "But you know what? I'll bet you're not the first to divorce your children."

"I can vouch for that," says Karen. "Not divorced, but abandoned. A little bit. For a little while."

"Did you abandon your children?" Gretchen asks, a little worried. Karen's oldest is only nine.

"No," says Karen. "Not me. Someone else."

"Someone in your husband's congregation?"

"Never mind," Karen says quickly. "I'm just saying that right when you think you're a horrible person for saying or doing something, you find out you're not alone."

"It is a comfort," Gretchen says. "Unless, you know, you're a mass murderer or something. Is there any more wine? To go with my whining?"

"You're *not whining*!" all the women say together, and Gretchen says, "Gosh, you guys. *Thank* you."

Experiments

✦

On Saturday morning, Nola comes into the kitchen, letting the screen door bang shut behind her, and Iris quickly checks to make sure the chocolate soufflé in the oven—the sample cake for her class later this morning—hasn't fallen. No, thank heavens. "Big news!" Nola says.

"Oh?" asks Maddy, who is sitting at the kitchen table reviewing a stack of old black-and-white photos she found at Time and Again, the basement thrift shop at St. Ignatius Church. They are inspiring her to go in a different direction with her own work. She told Iris she wants to focus on this small town and the people in it, as this unknown artist did, and that she has a lot of ideas about things she has seen that she would like to capture: Chairs on porches angled toward each other as though they are engaged in conversation. The line out the door of Sugarbutter at four-thirty in the afternoon, when they offer 75 percent off on what they haven't sold. The old man who walks down the block every morning with his hands clasped behind his back, a pack of four unleashed dachshunds following him. The loners on the elementary school playground who watch the others play—last week, Maddy told Iris, she saw a solemn little girl hiding in the bushes to watch, and had thought, *That was me.* She said she wished Iris had gotten a photo of Nola and Link splashing in the puddles that day they played in the rain.

Nola sits down on a kitchen chair turned backward, her chin resting on the top rail. This is new. She calls it "cowgirly." She wants to eat her meals this way, too, but Maddy forbids it.

"You might not believe this, but it's true," Nola says. "Link has found the formula to make a *mummy.*"

Iris takes off her apron and sits at the table. "Do tell."

Nola looks at her. "What?"

"Tell us!"

"Okay. So, what you do first is you get a dead thing. We used a goldfish from Link's friend. The fish died yesterday. Link was in Kenny's room and the fish was fine and then Kenny looked over and—*bang!*—the fish was floating upside down. And Kenny was all sad and crying and then Link said, 'But what if his death would contribute to a great scientific experiment—would you feel better then?' And his friend said no, but he said that Link could have the fish because he was only going to flush him, anyway. Fucillius, his name was, which I didn't even know that was a name. But Kenny gave the fish to Link and now we are finally going to make a mummy. That was our favorite experiment that we wanted to do." She looks at Iris. "Do we have any of those gingersnaps left?"

For a second, Iris thinks she means to use them to mummify something, then realizes the child just wants a cookie. "Okay?" Iris asks Maddy, and Maddy nods and says, "I'd like one, too," and Iris gets out three plates and three glasses and the carton of milk. She puts the cookie jar in the center of the table and peers in. "Two each," she says, and divides them.

"So how do you make a mummy?" she asks Nola.

Nola squints at her. "You might not like to eat at this next part because it is about you have to scrape all the fish's guts out. We had to use a grapefruit spoon, which, if you don't know, has these really sharp edges."

Iris pauses, but continues eating. Maddy, too. "Go ahead," she tells her daughter.

"You get all the guts out, and then you put a whole bunch of baking soda inside the fish, you push it in really tight. And then you put baking soda in the bottom of a container and lay the fish on top of it, and you put baking soda *over* him, too. And then you put the container away for a week." She bites into her second cookie and pours herself more milk.

Iris and Maddy sit silent, waiting. "And?" Iris finally says.

Nola waves her cookie. "And then we'll see. Because we just did that part, we put the container in his closet. But Link said in a week we'll take him out and put in more baking soda and then we wait another week and then he is supposed to be a mummy. See, the baking soda sucks up all his body's juices and he gets kind of leathery and that's what makes a mummy. Ta-da!"

"Nola, did you wash your hands after all this?" Maddy asks.

She sniffs her fingers delicately. "I think so. But don't worry—I didn't even help that much. I'm just the assistant. Next we are going to learn about crytojinctis."

"Cryogenics?" Iris asks.

"Oh. Right." She pushes herself back from the table. "Welp, I'm going up to read my book."

"Done playing with Link?" Maddy asks.

Nola turns around, smiling. "Ho! I would hang with him all day. But he is done with me for today. I'm too young for him anyway. Can I have *one* more cookie?" She holds up an index finger to emphasize the meagerness of her request.

"The cookies are all gone."

"Oh, yeah." She skips away.

Maddy watches her go. "I want to be like her when I grow up."

"Me, too," Iris says.

Maddy gets up to help clear the table. "Where's John lately?" she asks, her tone careful.

Iris shrugs. "Don't know. I tried calling him yesterday, but I don't think he charges his phone very regularly. Maybe I'll drive out to the farmhouse after class."

"And maybe I'll tell Matthew that Nola is starting summer school."

"Big doings in Mason," Iris says. "We might end up in the paper."

Maddy sits back down at the table. "Iris, have you talked to Abby lately?"

"No. Why?"

"I don't know. All these experiments Link is doing. I wonder if his mom's okay. I just keep thinking of how she almost died from leukemia. I wonder if she's had a recurrence."

Iris had started to reach into the cupboard for the flowered cake plates she wants to use for class. Now she turns to face Maddy.

"I mean, she's probably fine," Maddy says.

"But should we find out?" Iris asks.

"You do it," Maddy says. "You know her better."

"Yeah," Iris says, her mouth suddenly dry. It's true that she knows Abby better than Maddy does. But they're not close; Abby and Jason are very friendly, but private, people. Iris may know Abby better, but Maddy sees better. For example: *Where's John lately?*

Later in the morning, Iris goes next door to Abby and Jason's house. She is about to walk away, having both knocked and rung the doorbell without anyone answering. But then the door opens, and there is Abby before her, her purse on one shoulder, an overstuffed fabric bag on the other. "Oh!" she says. "Iris! Did you ring the bell? I'm sorry I didn't hear you; I had headphones on, and then I just grabbed all my stuff to rush out the door. But how are you?" She looks at the plate Iris is holding. "And what is *that* delicious-looking thing?"

"It's some chocolate soufflé. I just wanted to share a piece with you guys—it's awfully good." Then, "And also, I . . . Well, Maddy and I both were just wondering . . ."

Abby's face changes.

"I'm sorry if I'm intruding," Iris says.

"You're not exactly intruding. It's just that I wasn't going to tell everyone yet. But I guess you know, then, huh? How'd you find out?"

"It's just that Link has been doing all these experiments, and—"

Abby laughs. "Link and his experiments!"

Tears spring to Iris's eyes and she blinks them away.

Abby reaches out to touch her shoulder. "Are you okay?"

Is *she* okay? Iris waves her hand. "Allergies."

Abby looks at her watch. "I'm sorry, but I've got to get over to the bookstore. Link and Jason are there, but there's a lot to do. We're having an author event later this afternoon. A woman named Pamela Mills who writes poetry for children, and helps them to write their own. She also did that great book *Lucky Ducky*, such a sweet story. Do you know it?"

Iris shakes her head no.

"Well, it's about a duck who is lamenting the fact that he has nothing, and he comes to see that he has a lot. Not a very good synopsis, but it's a truly meaningful story for both kids and adults. The illustrations are superb, and she does them, too. Watercolors. I think a lot of people will come to the event because of that book, even though she wrote it years ago. I hope I can convince them to buy the new one."

"That's great, Iris. I know Maddy and Nola are coming. Can I help you carry your stuff out to the car?"

Abby looks at her fabric bag. "This? Oh, no, I'm fine. But thanks."

Abby starts down the walk, then turns around to Iris, still standing on the porch. "Will you put that cake in my refrigerator? The door's unlocked."

"I will!" Iris says.

Abby waves gaily, and Iris waves like her hand has been transformed into an overcooked noodle.

She goes into Abby's house and puts the cake in the refrigerator. There's a note anchored on the fridge door, next to a photo of Link lying in the grass in the backyard, reading, his dog, Hope, asleep beside him. DR. RICHARDS, MONDAY, 3 PM. BRING MEDS.

Poor Abby. Here she goes again. Iris looks around the kitchen: the chairs pulled up neatly to the table, the yellow curtains open, a wooden bowl of bananas and oranges and avocados centered on the table, a jar of almonds, half full, off to the side.

When Iris walks past the living room to let herself out, she sees books piled up here and there, invitingly. A collection of framed photos on an end table next to a white orchid. A pair of sneakers, the laces done up and lined up evenly, as though they are ready to take themselves out for a walk. A framed photo on the wall above the bookcase: the skyline of Chicago. A small oil painting on another wall of . . . what? She starts to move closer, then stops. She shouldn't be snooping this way.

Iris goes back home and finds her duck-shaped cookie cutters. She'll get some sugar cookies baked and decorated in less than an hour. Yellow cookies. Black eyes. Orange bills. A blue ribbon tied around each neck.

While the cookies are baking, she makes four ham sandwiches and puts them in a picnic basket. She adds the last of the cake, some bottles of iced tea and water, a container of leftover potato salad, another of coleslaw. Some cherry tomatoes. Two bananas, two oranges. In case he's hungry. In case she is. She'll drop the cookies off at the bookstore, then drive out to the farm with her hopeful little hamper.

In the car on the way to the bookstore, she thinks of Abby, going on with her life in spite of everything. She recalls a time she was a young girl, lying on the floor of her grandmother's living room with her cousin Timothy. The adults had gathered in the kitchen for coffee and conversation; she and Timothy were given paper for making drawings. Her cousin was drawing a fighter pilot, he said. The plane was in the middle of the page, and the rest of the page was full of bullets falling like rain. Iris didn't have a good feeling about the pilot's survival. Neither did Timothy, apparently; he told Iris, "This guy's going down."

Iris studied the pilot's round face, small-seeming inside his aviator's cap. He was looking out the plane's side window directly at his audience. Two black dots for eyes. A straight line for a nose. And a huge smile, many square teeth showing.

"Why is he *smiling*?" Iris asked, and Timothy drew back from his drawing and surveyed it. "It makes him feel better," he said.

Iris then returned to her own drawing: A house with a fence and a garden and a vase of roses in the window. A bird on a tree limb right outside the house, singing. She remembers she drew the notes the bird was singing, too. Nothing left to chance in Iris's world!

Another memory, more recent, of a friend in Boston who died of ovarian cancer. A few days after her diagnosis, Iris took her out for a drink. "What can I do for you?" Iris asked. And Hannah said, "Treat me like before."

So. Okay. She'll drop off the cookies, nothing but smiles for Abby. She'll buy a copy of the duck book to have signed. There'll be someone to give it to; there's always someone to give something good to.

The Gift of Rain

John switches the long blade of sweetgrass from one side of his mouth to the other. Three red-winged blackbirds are lined up on a branch of the river birch above him and they suddenly rise up together and fly away. Gone to roost. Dusk has arrived, and is bringing out colors one by one, the way it always does. He looks up into the trees above him, lets his eyes rove slowly over the leaves. He lingers on a bouquet-like grouping, where the last bit of sun illuminates their edges. And then, sitting just above those leaves, he sees an owl. The bird is motionless but for the blinking of its round eyes. Such sorrow in those eyes, if you ask John. Such acceptance. The owl sits, and only sits. A Buddha.

The gifts of the out-of-doors. Even on the streets of Chicago in bitter winter, he preferred being outside. The people he ran with, they all did. Most of the homeless did. Easier to have sex, should the occasion present itself, without worrying about some supervisor happening upon you.

And outside could hold more: tents and gigantic card-board boxes that began to feel like luxury accommodations, with their relative privacy and their walls decorated with images torn from magazines or with disintegrating photos. Outside could hold more bags full of belongings and food; it could also hold more despair and confusion and anger—such emotions needed room. If you felt things roiling up inside you, you weren't trapped a foot away from someone else. You could *move*.

But here, being outside is like being in a cathedral. He watches as a full moon materializes, a thin black cloud draped upon it like a celestial negiligee. Then he sits up, wraps his arms around his knees, and listens to the creek run.

He would like to stay here. He can be outside and be safe, and he can also have board-and-brick shelter when he needs it. But he's not sure he can stay. No one has bothered him yet, but he knows he's been seen. By Iris, of course, but also by a group of young men who tramped across the backyard recently and saw him in the kitchen. It probably won't be long until word spreads and someone shows up to kick him out, if not arrest him.

He came out to lie by the creek late this afternoon after he'd restuffed his mattress with some of the ancient hay from the loft in the barn, still good-smelling, if a bit dusty. He'd also worked on trying to repair the stairs in the house, or at least make them safer. He used a fine, weighty hammer he'd bought at the hardware store and a half-full box of nails he'd found at the dump. He used boards that were left at a curb where workmen were rebuilding a house; they had welcomed John to them. They had also agreed to letting him work for them for cash next week. A lucky day, that one.

After repairing the stairs, John had tended to his garden: weeding, staking, burying eggshells and coffee grounds at the base of the tomato plants, turning the earth to aerate it and to bring up some worms for the birds.

He was weary, then, and he'd lain in the tall weeds, listening to the breeze making card-ruffling sounds in the leaves of the tree above him. He'd fallen asleep, and for the first time in a long time, he'd awakened from a bad dream. Vietnam, again, the long fingers of that awful time still able to reach out and grab him: Men wearing necklaces made of ears they'd severed from dead VC. The SOP corralling of frightened old men in the villages they burned, their thin beards trembling, their legs trembling, their hands. The young mothers holding babies, crying, the mothers of those young mothers dead-eyed, resigned to their fate. They had done nothing. Didn't matter.

He might have yelled or screamed in the dream—he doesn't know. Proud Mary told him once that he always cried out in his sleep. He doesn't think he *always* did; but what does he know?

Poor Mary. He wonders about her. He worries about her. But he can't go back to her, even in memory. Move on. It's the only thing he does well.

Although it must be allowed that his skills as a handy-man are improving. At the dump, he found a book called *Chix Can Fix*. Title notwithstanding, he brought it home and studied it. Some of the things in there he already knew: drywall repair, removing a P trap, adjusting a strike plate; many, he did not. He put an ad up on a grocery store bulletin board for small fix-it jobs. Lo and behold, the next day, he got called by one Ollie Futters. He put in a new flapper in her toilet, fixed a jammed garbage disposal, and replaced a rotting board on the front porch. He has a date to paint the porch next week. White, except for the ceiling, which Ollie wants painted robin's-egg blue. She's got to be near ninety, living all alone, but doing just fine. Just as John was leaving, her ride came to pick her up for her weekly trip to Save More. The driver was named Tiny Dawson and it appeared he pretty much had the cab market sewn up in Mason. He gave John a ride to the grocery store so that his hitch back to the farm would be shorter, after making sure it was okay with Ollie. ("For heaven's sake, do you even have to ask?" was her reply. And then, "What's the difference if one more is along? Put him in the back and let me ride up front! Stuff another one in, if you want, *I* don't care.")

Tiny was a really nice guy, and his wife, Monica, owns Polly's Henhouse. John knows her, that fair-complexioned, black-haired woman with the sweet expression who is not about to take crap from anyone. He heard Tiny tell the old lady that Monica was in her last trimester now, and doing fine. That put him in mind of things he didn't want to think about ever again.

On the same bulletin board where John posted his notice, he saw an ad for a dog-walking service looking for help. He could handle that, but there'd be forms to fill out, his history dug into. He doesn't want to deal with any of that ever again. He collects no Social Security. He renews minutes on cheap phones whenever he has enough cash.

He gets up, stretches, and starts back toward the house. He's got some beans, some brown bread, a tomato, a Snickers bar. Just as he's going in the back door, he hears a car pulling into the driveway. He walks around front, and sees Iris stepping from her car, carrying a picnic basket. "Are you hungry?" she asks.

He hasn't called her since that glorious day. He hasn't returned her calls. He's been afraid to. But here she is. Not afraid of his afraid.

He thinks of his mother as she lay dying, also unafraid. John was fifteen years old, sitting on the floor beside her bed. He didn't know what to do. He didn't know what to say. And so he simply sat, listening to her breathe, listening to the things she occasionally whispered to him when she rose to consciousness. "I'm all right, son, don't you worry," she said.

"I know where I'm going." She said that a lot, and usually she smiled when she said it. "Be a kind man," she told him, many times. That and "Have hope."

Hope, he thought. He wondered what kind of hopes his mother had in marrying the man who backed her into the corners, away from the windows, to slap her. Who dragged her from her bed one night and threw her out into the snow in her nightgown. Locked the door and laughed. Then let her in and lay on top of her on the living room floor, eight-year-old John sitting at the top of the stairs, his fist in his mouth, his chest heaving. It was after that incident that his mother finally got the wherewithal to throw his father out. But then they were poorer than ever, and John's mother had to work two jobs. He kept the house key in his lunchbox and told no one that he returned from school to an empty house where he spent such long hours alone.

One of the last things his mother said to him was "Take risks, Johnny. Taking risks is just unmasking hope, you know. Things don't always work out in this world. But they do often enough." With no small effort, she raised herself up on one elbow. "'Tis how I got you, by taking a risk. And it was worth it, so it was."

"Seriously, I've got a lot of food in here," Iris says. "Want some?"

He comes back into the present like a man falling from the sky. He stares at Iris. "Yes," he says.

A woman in a white summer dress, a scarf in her long hair. Little pearl earrings like orbs of moon.

As she walks toward him, fat raindrops start to fall, and

there is a sudden smell of rust in the air. Startled, they both look up at the sky.

"You always bring the rain, Iris. Are you a witch, then?"

"Sometimes," she says. And then, touching his arm, "It's nice to see you. I've missed you."

A woman in a white summer dress, a scarf in her hair, curls damp at her temples. A woman smelling like flowers and like sun and now like rain, too. A woman whose skin might as well be made of velvet, whose heart seems open and unfettered.

"I've missed you, too," he tells her, and his voice is very quiet. He clears his throat and speaks louder. "I've missed you but I was afraid to ask you to come. But here you are." He shakes his head slowly, as if in wonder. "Thank you."

John has always been able to attract women. From the time he was a boy, he's been complimented on his looks. He is still a good-looking man, he knows. And he knows he has a certain charm. He has used it often enough, for a specific kind of comfort. But this woman Iris has made her way into a different place inside him.

A buddy he knew in 'Nam, Tim Glasser, was hospitalized not long after they both got home. Colon cancer. The night before his surgery, John went to visit Tim, who had a wife and a four-month-old baby. He told John, "I never was as scared in Vietnam as I am now." John had nodded. He was still with Laura, then, and their new baby, and the thought of ever losing them was paralyzing. Tim's treatment was successful, and on the day he was discharged, John went to pick him up. Before they left the room, the men wept in each other's arms. A couple of months later, Laura took the baby and left. Restraining order, the whole nine yards. One time too many, which is to say three times, he'd awakened in the middle of the night and tried to strangle his wife, thinking she was VC. After the second time, Laura told him he had to go for counseling. He went once, then never went back. He couldn't do it. He couldn't say those things and he couldn't hear those things. Not yet. Not yet, he kept telling her. And so one morning he came downstairs to a note on the kitchen table, and to the utter and complete silence of these new bombs falling all around him.

But now he holds out his hand to Iris, and she takes it and follows him around back. Before they reach the door, she slips in the mud that has already formed, and falls flat on her behind. "Oh, jeez," she says, laughing. He sits on the earth beside her and, while the thunder rumbles low in the distance, pulls her to him and kisses her again and again.

They have finished eating the oranges, and the peels lie in fragrant, loose circles on Iris's belly. She is lying flat on John's bed, and he is on his side, resting his head on one hand and looking down at her. The evening has gone lazy and expansive. They've talked about many things, including his time in Vietnam: the absurdity of the mission; the constant fear that was abated only by something worse, a sudden lack of caring anymore what happened to anyone, including himself; the treatment of the vets who came home to an ungrateful nation, especially contrasted with the applause and special benefits service people experienced these days. Now he says, "I don't believe it's ever going to be anything people can really understand unless they were there. But for some of us, there's no escape. For some of us . . ." He shrugs. "Some of us came to Vietnam with nothing to grab on to when the shit came down. You know what I'm saying?"

She nods. He'd told her quite a bit about his growing-up years, too.

"Ever since I came home, I haven't been able to quite make sense of things the way I used to. I haven't had any desire to sort of incorporate myself into the lives I see being lived around me. I don't . . . *agree*. I don't have the same values. I don't have the same wants and needs as most of the people I see around me. I don't care about what they care about. I don't know what I want, but I know what I *don't* want.

"Despite the way I was raised, I believed for a long time that people were fundamentally good. That life might be hard but it was full of promise and reward. My mother gave me that. With her, I felt like I was hiding in a corner with her protecting me with one arm and with the other pointing to a place beyond where we were now, where it was good. Where things were possible. After she died, I still believed in that promise. After I went to 'Nam, I didn't believe it anymore." He grows quiet, a bitter flame reignited; he's sure she can hear it in his voice. She lies still beside him.

"I've seen the devil and the devil is all of us," he tells her, finally.

"I believe you," she says. "I think that, too, except that I would say that the devil is all of us and the angels are, too. And life is nothing if not having to choose who's in charge."

"Sometimes you don't get a choice." His voice is louder now.

"Maybe sometimes you don't see it." Her voice is even. "Maybe sometimes you need to purposefully focus on all the beauty around you."

He picks up an orange peel and lays it just below her collarbone. "Can you smell that?"

"Yes. So?"

"So maybe you're right, and now we can talk about that beautiful scent rather than the time I was hacking through the jungle, first guy on the line, and the kid behind me comes up and says, 'Let me do that—you're beat.' I was beat, and I fell back and let him do it. Two more steps, and he's hit by a sniper. His best friend runs over to try to help him and he gets taken out by a claymore. It sounds like a shot, but then there's a massive explosion, big red fire cloud. And I'm standing there with M&M's in my rucksack that I'd intended to share with those kids that night, I liked those kids. As it was, I ate them alone. They weren't there, so I ate them all." He holds the peel under his nose. "But. The scent of an orange! All better."

"I didn't say that," Iris says, and now he sees her anger mounting. "Don't belittle me."

"What did you say, then?"

"I guess I said there are *alternatives* to certain ways of *thinking*. And there are people who want to *help*."

"Oh, Iris. Don't try to help me. Please don't do that."

She sits up and reaches for her clothes. He puts his hand firmly over hers.

She turns to face him. "Let go of my hand."

Now they are two different people.

He lets go of her, looks down. "I'm sorry. I only don't want you to go quite yet. I'm sorry."

She stands to dress, says nothing. Slips on her sandals. Heads for the door.

"Iris," he says.

She goes outside. He hears the car door slam and the ignition turn over, then cut out. Then, nothing. He imagines the stars looking down on her, saying, rightly, *Leave. Get away from him.*

He goes to the kitchen and sits naked at the table, lights a candle.

And she comes back in.

"Iris," he says. "I'm sorry."

"*I'm* sorry," she says. "I shouldn't have asked you so much about it." There is nothing but calm in her eyes. Women are always the brave ones. John's been feeding a cardinal couple sunflower seeds he buys at the hardware store. Always, it's the female who comes first to the jar lid he's nailed to a fence post near the place where John likes to sit. The male will watch nervously for a while, like an avian Don Knotts, until he finally ventures over.

"I shouldn't have pushed you to talk about it," she says.

He rubs one eye hard, leans back in his chair, and smiles up at her.

"Do-overs?"

She comes to sit opposite him. "It's just that I want to know you. I really do."

For this he has no answer. The flame gutters, then grows tall and steady, and they both regard it as though it, too, has spoken.

"Let's go back to my house for a while," Iris says.

Everything in him lines up to say no. *Nope!* But look here: he stands, then looks down at himself. "Might be better if I go dressed. And I got a new comb yesterday, so I'll give it a try-out. Have some tea while you wait, Iris. Make yourself comfortable."

"I am comfortable," she says, looking right at him.

"I'm glad for both of us then," he says, but the truer mouth that is his brain says, *Ah, no. Don't be. You won't be for long.*

The conversation they have in the car on the way to Iris's house is a kind of walking on ice; it's careful that way. But it is kind. And hopeful.

"How are the baking classes going?" he asks.

"Oh, tomorrow is a really popular class: homemade dog biscuits."

"Really?"

"Really. We have three varieties: peanut butter, bacon, and peanut butter and bacon. And a nice variety of cookie cutters, too. A bone, of course. But also fire hydrants and balls and all kinds of dogs."

"No cats?" John asks. "Or rolled-up newspapers? Or slippers?"

"Not yet. But that's a good idea. In the morning, Nola will write the copy; she likes to do that. 'Fluffy will flip for these!' That sort of thing. For tonight, I need to make up some sample biscuits. Want to help me?"

"I'm your man."

Well, too much, that one. They ride the rest of the way in silence.

After John leaves, Maddy and Iris sit on the front porch. "I like John a lot," Maddy says, and Iris says, "Umm."

"You do, too, right?"

"I don't know. I guess I do. Yes. I do."

"Nola's nuts about him," Maddy says. "I kind of love that they went outside and lay in the backyard together."

"You didn't worry?" Iris asks.

"What do you mean?"

"It didn't make you nervous that she was alone with him?"

"They were right in the backyard. Which is fenced. I could see them out there. He was showing her constellations."

Iris nods. "Okay."

Now Maddy straightens and faces her. "Why? Were you worried? Is there something I should know? Should I not let Nola be alone with him? Oh, my God, you should have told me!"

"No, no," Iris says. "It's not that. I think he really loves kids. They certainly seem to respond to him. It's just that . . . he is complicated."

"In what way?"

"He's pretty damaged—let's just say that."

Maddy laughs, a bitter sound. "Yeah, there's a lot of us in that club."

Iris looks over at her. "Are you . . . Is there anything you want to talk about?"

"I found out today that Nola has been secretly talking to Matthew. On Link's phone."

"Really? Why on Link's phone?"

"That's what I asked her. She said it seemed like I didn't want her to talk to Matthew. I said that wasn't true, that I didn't mind her talking to him. She said, 'Well, you're always listening, like prison, and your face gets all frown-y when I talk to him. And I don't get any privacy. Even if you leave the room, you listen. I see your shadow. And some things are just private.'"

"Like *prison*?" Iris says, and laughs in spite of herself.

"Yeah," Maddy says, and she, too, smiles. "I guess she's right. I do worry about her talking to Matthew."

"What are you afraid of, do you think?" Iris asks.

Maddy sighs. "That he's given up on me. And he's just waiting for the right time to tell me."

"You need to be honest with him about what's going on with you," Iris says. "You're not being fair."

"I know that. I owe it to him and I owe it to Nola, too. Matthew's not Nola's biological father, but he's her father anyway."

"Then *tell* him, Maddy! Tell him you want to move back here!"

"Well, I called him today to do just that and he didn't pick up on the house phone or the cell. Called him a couple of times more and then I left a message and he didn't call back."

"Oh," Iris says. "Well. That doesn't mean he won't."

"Right." Maddy stands up. "It's late. I'm going to bed."

"Me, too," Iris says. She and Maddy go into the kitchen and see the light in the kitchen next door go off. For a moment, they both stand there. Then, "Has Link said anything to Nola?" Iris asks.

"You mean, about his mom?"

Iris nods.

"Not that I know of. I think she'd tell me if he did. I think she'd have some questions."

"Don't we all," says Iris.

Eeenie Meenie Miney Mo

※

When Iris awakens, she sits for a while at the edge of the bed. The house is quiet; she guesses Maddy and Nola have gone out. She's thinking about the turn the conversation took with John when they were at the farmhouse. She's not sure these kinds of things won't happen more often, his mood descending into a place where she can't reach him. It's an uneasy, disappointed feeling she has, and the level of her disappointment makes it clear how invested she is in him. In them. But then she reasons that no relationship is perfect, and he certainly has justification for being the way that he is. People overcome things. Love heals. She believes this wholeheartedly.

She showers, dresses, eats a light breakfast, and then sits at her desk to answer emails and place orders for her baking classes: the requisite flour and sugar, more bars of baking chocolate, a large bottle of vanilla paste, nonpareils. There is an email from Tailwaggers, a rescue site she went to last week, just to see what dogs were available. She loves her cat, but she has wanted a dog (as well as every other animal under the sun) since she was a child. Why not get one now? She works from home; her cat, Homer, gets along with the dog next door and there's no reason to think he wouldn't adapt to a new member of the family. Maddy, Nola, and Link would all help her with walking. The email is informing her that a new litter of puppies is now available for adoption. The puppies—there are seven of them—are a Great Pyrenees mix, and each is cuter than the last: brown-and-white, freckle-faced, fluffy coats, gigantic paws, that endearing look of puppy dopiness on their faces. Iris goes downstairs and grabs her car keys: she'll go and just look at them. On the way, she'll stop at a pet store, because who does she think she's fooling? She'll have time to get a harness, a leash, some toys, and puppy food. Surely some of the puppies will still be there when she gets to the shelter. Nonetheless, her tires squeal backing out of the driveway.

Two and a half hours later, Iris carries the puppy she chose—a female the shelter had named Angel—out to her car, wrapped in a soft blanket. She uses the seatbelt to anchor the crate she bought on the seat beside her, then puts the puppy in it. The dog immediately lies down, her nose on her paws. Iris guesses she's tired; she and two of her littermates spent a long time playing with Iris before she finally chose Angel. It is in the back of her mind to come back and get the other two tomorrow. If not later tonight.

She heads toward home, but then turns the car around to head to the farm. She'll show John first. She'll let the puppy play on the open land.

When she pulls up to John's house, she sees him coming out the door. She leans her head out the window. "Hey!"

He raises his hand.

"Are you going somewhere?"

"Not anymore." He walks over to the car, sees the crate. "Look at that," he says, smiling. "Is it yours?"

"I just got her," Iris says. "Okay if I let her run around?"

"Of course!" He opens the side door to get the puppy out of the crate and lowers her gently to the ground. She stands looking up at him. He pets her, then takes a few steps back. The dog follows. Then he turns and runs, and the dog follows. Iris laughs, and the joy she is feeling seems caught in her throat.

"Angel!" she says, and the dog runs to her.

"That her name?" John asks.

"That's what the shelter named her."

"Hm."

"Got a better idea?"

He looks at the dog. "Not yet."

He lies on the ground and the dog is all over him. *Nothing like a puppy to make you young again*, Iris thinks.

"You're not going to keep her in the crate, are you?" John asks.

"Not all the time."

He says nothing, and Iris says, "Why? Do you not like crates for dogs?"

"I don't like crates for anything."

Iris nods. She doesn't, either, actually.

"Let her out every couple of hours, take up her water a bit before she goes to sleep for the night, you'll house-train her in no time. You don't need a crate." He leans forward deferentially. "Of course, she's not my dog. It's just my opinion."

"I'll take all the help I can get. I've never had a dog."

John frowns. "Never had a dog!"

"Nope. My mother wouldn't let me have any pets."

"People have burned in hell for less."

Iris laughs.

"I've had a lot of dogs," John says. "I can teach them tricks fast as Jimmy's ashes. You want this dog to learn to sit in five minutes?"

"Yes!"

"Did you buy some treats?"

"Yes! In fact, they're called 'Train Me.'"

"All right, we'll teach her 'sit.' And we'll teach her 'come'—that's important. No more for today; you can't overload them. But I'll tell you, growing up, I taught my dogs to fetch the newspapers, to roll over three times, to wait for their dinners, to smile. I taught them to pray!"

"How'd you teach them to *pray*?" Iris asks.

"Oh, that's easy. Tell them to sit. Front paws up on a chair before them. Then nose down to the paws, eyes raised up imploringly."

"Do you think they liked doing it?"

"Well, their tails would be going a mile a minute. Dogs live to please you, Iris. Just don't ever take advantage of that. And never hit this dog—you know that, right? Not with a newspaper, not with your hand—don't ever hit her."

"I . . . Okay. I mean, I wasn't planning on it."

"You never have to hit. You never have to yell at them, either. They're sensitive creatures, like most children are. They'll love you no matter what." He shrugs. "Kind of breaks your heart, really."

Like most *animals* are, Iris thinks he means, but she doesn't correct him.

He gets up, brushes himself off. "All right then, Angel. Are you ready for lesson one?"

The dog tugs at his shoelace, and John picks her up. "Ah, we can do better than shoelaces now, can't we?" He walks toward the backyard, and calls over his shoulder for Iris to follow.

When they reach the pasture fence, John rolls up his sleeves.

"There were two of her littermates left," Iris says.

"Were there?"

"Yup. Think we should add to the family?"

John's demeanor changes as suddenly as if cold water has just been poured over him. He stiffens, takes a step back. His shoulders hunch and his hands slide slowly into his pockets.

Now I've done it, Iris thinks. *Now I've done something.*

"Just kidding," she says, and John nods. Then he reaches out for the bag of treats Iris is holding.

"First thing is, you give them a sample of what they've got coming," he says, and offers the puppy a treat. She gobbles it down, then looks up at him. Barks.

"Smart dog," John says. Bending down toward the puppy, he says, "But we're doing 'sit' now. We'll do 'speak' later, okay, lassie?" He looks up at Iris. "You can't rush things."

"No," Iris says. "I know."

Do You See What I See?

"All right, I'm just going to say it," Dodie says. "I might be dating an exhibitionist."

Silence at the table. And then Joanie says, "What?"

"Well, maybe I should give some background first. Even though it's pretty embarrassing."

"The background?" Toots asks. Then, because the women are beginning to talk among themselves, she says loudly, "Order!" Then, again, to Dodie, "The *background* is embarrassing?"

"Right."

"Not the fact that you're dating an exhibitionist? Is it a *real* one?"

"Let her talk!" says Karen. "After I get more wine. Wow, I can't wait to hear this one."

"You're a *preacher*'s wife!" says Rosemary.

"Right," says Karen. "Emphasis on *wife*, not preacher. I *am* my own person, you know. Everybody always forgets that. I am not my husband. And I actually am interested in . . . all kinds of things!" She runs to the kitchen for another bottle of wine, then comes back and says breathlessly, "Go ahead."

Dodie takes in a breath. "Okay. Does anyone here watch *The Bachelorette*?"

A few women murmur assent.

"I never watched it until recently. But now I am absolutely addicted. I would never tell anyone but you all this, but I get positively enraged if I get interrupted when I'm watching."

"You should tape it," says Maddy. "Then you can pause it."

"I watch it on demand," says Dodie. "I *can* pause it. But I get aggravated if I have to pause it!"

"Wow," Maddy says.

"See what I mean?" Dodie says, and no one says yes. She continues, "I started watching it as a kind of joke. I'd heard about the Becca disaster, how this young girl was dumped in such a humiliating way by her fiancé. But now she was coming back to the show and this time *she* would be the one choosing, and I thought, 'Oh for heaven's sake, they put the most ridiculous things on television these days.' But I'm telling you, it's like hypnosis. I get positively transfixed. I love the outfits, especially those sparkly evening gowns that nobody wears anymore. I like to see where they go on their dates, and—oh!—When they have the rose ceremonies? I'm on the edge of my seat. Literally!

Once I leaned so far in, I spilled my wine all over my rug. Red wine, too! But I get so involved! That episode where Colton went home, and he kissed Becca's *hand* when he said goodbye? Oh, that poor boy. I just bawled, watching him sitting in that limo trying to pull himself together. And the fact that he was a virgin! A professional football player who's a virgin? Imagine! I mean, I had to ask myself: Is that an attractive quality or not? Wouldn't it get tiresome having to teach him everything? Or would it be the sweetest thing that he hadn't ever done it? He *would* come with a clean bill of health, STD-wise. But anyway, the point is, because of that show I am having the weirdest fantasies. I even fantasize that they come up with a version for seniors, and I get to be on it. *I'm* the Bachelorette!"

"I have fantasies about being on *The Voice*," Karen says. "Nobody knows this, but I actually have a good voice. Sometimes I sing in the shower and pretend I'm auditioning and all the chairs turn for me."

Joanie says, "I have that exact same fantasy! And then after the chairs turn and they say, 'What's your name?' I say, 'My name is Joanie Benson, I'm from Mason, Missouri, I'm a retired librarian, and I'm sixty-five years old,' and the audience goes crazy."

"Let's stay focused on Dodie here," Toots says. "So, Dodie, you're having fantasies of dating an exhibitionist?"

"I'm *getting* there," Dodie says. "The point of my telling you about that TV show is that it rekindled things in me that I thought were long dead. I got all dreamy-eyed, sitting with my morning coffee, imagining this and that. So one day I'm sitting there and I see across the way into the kitchen of the house next door and there's Albert McIntosh, my neighbor. His wife died a year ago and he's been a hermit. Just devastated, I guess. But there he is at his big kitchen window that faces my house, and he is in the altogether. I could see *every*thing, okay? I'm talking full frontal. And then he saw me looking at him and he just . . . well, he just stood there."

"Ew," says Karen. "That's disgusting."

"No," Dodie says. "That's not how I felt. I mean, I know how it sounds. You think of him as a dirty old man, Karen. You look at all those buff guys at the gym and you forget about *real* bodies. And don't forget, you're still young. If you got divorced, you could find someone else easily, if you wanted to. You'd have a lot of men to choose from.

"At my age, I can't afford to be picky. And I can take chances I never did before. What the heck! I know Albert. He's a nice guy. I don't *mind* if he's a bit of an exhibition-ist. Maybe he's just proud that he's held up so well. He has held up well. At this age, you figure there's going to be something wrong with everyone and I'd rather he be a bit of an exhibitionist than pick at his teeth in public. Also, he might just be one of those guys who sleeps nude and he got up and he was standing by the window and he saw me and I didn't freak out so he didn't run away and hide. And you know what? You know what? And I guess here's the real confession: the next day I came down into the kitchen in my sheer yellow nightie that I haven't worn in I'll bet forty-five years. And I went to the window and waited for him to come into his kitchen naked again. After a few minutes, he did. And he looked at me and I looked at him and then he waved and then I waved and then I lifted my gown. I did! I flashed him! And then we both started laughing. And he pointed to his backyard, like, would I meet him out there?"

"*Naked?*" Karen asks.

"No!" Dodie says. "He had on a pair of nice khaki pants and a turquoise-blue Izod shirt and he looked very nice. And I had on my floral-print summer dress with the lace collar and then just my Keds because I'm damned if I can wear any cute shoes anymore.

"When we met outside, we didn't say anything about . . . We just started talking and then he invited me to dinner and then that night he came home with me and, well, there's still lead in the pistol, if you catch my drift."

"You *did* it?" Gretchen asks.

"In a *manner of speaking*, and that's all I'm saying. That's my confession: I am dating an exhibitionist. Or maybe a nudist. And I like it. And I don't care. And I am happy."

"He's not really an exhibitionist," Toots says. "He just got caught naked. And then you made the most of it. Right?"

"I guess," Dodie says. She looks at her watch. "So that's all I got. Someone else could go."

"Anyone have anything?" Toots asks. "Or should we adjourn?"

Iris raises her hand. "I'm in love with a homeless man."

"You mean that real handsome guy living on the old Dooley farm?" Toots asks. "He's a very nice man, apparently. Just . . . homeless. Poor thing."

Small towns, Iris thinks. It really is true that everyone knows everything. "Have you seen him?" she asks.

"I know about him. He's about to get kicked off the place—I heard the police talking about him at the town council meeting last week. Unless he wants to buy it. They're going to offer to let him buy it. It's for sale, real cheap. The only surviving family lives out in Oregon and they're tired of paying taxes. They'll sell it for ten thousand dollars."

"Really?" Iris asks. Beside her, Maddy stiffens. *I'm not going to buy it!* Iris wants to tell her. But the truth is, she might.

A Discovery

❦

The morning that John comes to paint the ceiling of Ollie Futters's porch, she tells him she's sorry but she's changed her mind.

"That's okay," he says, and starts to walk away.

"Where are you going?" she asks.

He turns around. "I thought you changed your mind."

"About the *color*. I don't want just blue. I want stars up there, too. Gold stars, and if they are glittery, all the better. Do you think they make glittery gold paint?"

"Pretty sure they do," John says. "Seems like they make just about every kind of paint imaginable. I'll go to the store and see."

"No, no, not today," Ollie says. "Just do the blue today. You can come back tomorrow and do the stars, unless you're busy. That way, I get to see you two days in a row, don't you know." She tilts her head and smiles.

"I'm not busy," he says. Even if he were, he'd ac-

commodate Ollie. He likes and admires her. She still
grows her own tomatoes and pole beans. She is relent-
lessly optimistic. She uses her magnifying glass to read
the paper every day. She wears a White Sox cap even
though she's a Cardinals fan because she feels bad for
the way people in Chicago fawn all over the Cubs. "Lovable losers, my eye," she told John. She keeps her bird
feeders full and she has a little band of feral cats that
come around twice a day to eat, and Ollie claims they all
know which dish is theirs. "I got a tough old yellow tom
gets beat up every night, I swear," she told John. "And
you know what bowl he likes? The flowered one. Isn't
that something? Poor guy. His left ear is holding on with
spit and a prayer. I'd like to take him to Dr. Thomas. He
is just the best vet ever, he came over here to send my
sweet golden retriever Breezy over the Rainbow Bridge.
She got to be in her own bed when she died and she
wasn't afraid. Fourteen years old—it was her time, but
I just cried and cried and Dr. Thomas sat with me and
patted my hand and when I finally stopped crying, he
wrapped Breezy up in her blanket and put her ever so
gently in the back of his van. And then he told me, he
said, 'Let's take Breezy for one last car ride,' and we went
over to Willigan's and he bought me a hot-fudge sundae
and then drove me home and he said, 'Now, you watch
something funny on television. You gave Breezy a perfect
life.'"

Ollie grows quiet for a moment, tearful, but then she laughs. "That old tomcat would have a fit if I tried to touch him. I'm growing on him, though. I can tell. Won't be long and he'll be right up on my lap."

After John has applied the blue paint, he knocks on the door to tell Ollie he's leaving. "Come in for a minute," she says. "I want to show you something I found online."

She shuffles over to her little desk and shows him an image on the screen of her computer. Her godson got her all set up on the computer as a birthday present recently, and she's justifiably proud of the skills she's acquired from classes at the library. "I want the stars just like that," she says, and points to a porch ceiling, painted black, stars everywhere. "I found this on Pinterest."

"But you want a blue ceiling, right?" he says.

"Right. Best of both worlds. Why not? We might could put Breezy up there, too. With a halo."

They hear a *ping* and Ollie opens an email. "Oh, look! Someone tagged me on Facebook! Shall we see what they said?"

"Sure," John says.

Ollie navigates to Facebook and leans forward with her magnifying glass to read the message. "Well, Monica Dawson over at the Henhouse has put my picture up on their customer wall of fame. Wonder what I'm famous for. Being old, I guess. But isn't that nice? I'll have to look for it next time I go in." She turns in her chair. "Are you on Facebook, John?"

He laughs. "No." He did at one time use it, to keep in touch with guys from his unit in Vietnam. But it seemed pointless after a while, so he stopped.

"You can find *everyone* online," Ollie says. "Dead or alive. Give me a name, I'll show you."

He says it before he can stop himself: "Laura Cox." Surely she would have gone back to her maiden name.

Ollie types it in, then leans back triumphantly. Slowly, she scrolls through the faces. "Are any of these her?"

"No," John says. And then, his throat dry, he says, "Would you try Laura Loney?"

Ollie types it in, and there she is—one of those women is his Laura. "That one," John says. "Can you click on her?"

Ollie does, and lands on Laura's Facebook page. Her hair has gone gray, her face has filled out. But there she is, her smile still so genuine, her gaze so direct. She is standing with a man who looks to be in his late forties. Their son? Must be. He looks like John—his eyes, his chin. Only he looks happy. Unbroken.

"Is she married?" he asks. "Can you see if she's married?"

Ollie leans in to look and says, "Says here she's single. Pretty little thing, isn't she? Who is she?"

"Just . . . a cousin," John says. "I was always fond of her."

He shoves his hands in his pockets. "I'll go and get your gold paint."

Also, he'll stop by the library. One way or another, he'll find Laura's address.

They'll help you with everything there. You just have to ask.

Decisions

❧

The kitchen door is open to admit a cool evening breeze, and a cardinal in a nearby tree is whistling so loudly it's as though it's asking to come in. Iris and Maddy are sitting at the kitchen table tasting the lemon ricotta cookies Iris has baked for her class tomorrow: A Lotta Ricotta, it's called, and it features these cookies; ricotta mousse with balsamic-pepper cherries; ricotta doughnuts; ricotta ice cream; and—best of all, as Iris sees it—a recipe for making your own ricotta. Teach a man to fish. "Delicious!" Maddy says, wiping a crumb from the corner of her mouth.

"I don't know," Iris says. "I feel like they need to be tarter."

"Put in more lemon juice?"

"Then the dough will be too wet."

"Add more flour, too?"

"Then they'll be too dry."

The women sit quietly, thinking, and then Iris says,

"Oh, for Pete's sake. I know this one. Citric acid! I'll add it to the recipe."

"Oh, yeah!" Maddy says. "Lucille used that in her lemon meringue pie. She always said, 'If lemon meringue pie doesn't make you pucker so hard your eyes cross, feed it to your garbage disposal.'"

The screen door bangs open and Nola comes into the kitchen with the puppy, Lassie, followed closely by Link. "What smells so good?" she asks, unleashing the dog. The puppy gets a long drink of water, then collapses on the fluffy rug Iris keeps under the table for her.

"Lemon ricotta cookies," Maddy says. "Want some?"

"Later," Nola says. "We have to do an experiment now, and Abby is waiting."

"What experiment?" Iris asks.

Link comes over to the table and sits down, and Iris resists an impulse to push his red hair out of his eyes. He's got the best-looking freckles, the bluest eyes. And she thinks he's one of the kindest, most sensitive children she's ever met. "Well," he says, eyeing the cookies, "it's not *exactly* an experiment. But my mom has a question, and I found this thing you can do to get the answer."

Iris looks over at Maddy. Only last night, Iris told Maddy that Abby believed in being really honest with children; she'd told Iris that not long after they first met. And now Iris wonders if the question Abby has is about whether the new treatments will work or not. Thus far, the women have seen no change in Abby, except for fatigue. It's hard to think, though, that such important and fearsome questions would be handled in this way: a whimsical experiment, conducted by children, to speak to such a serious concern?

On the other hand, why not be direct about these things, even with, or perhaps especially with, your children? If you're not afraid, if you face things straight on, mightn't it help them? When Maddy went to the book signing for *Lucky Ducky*, she had seen a book called *My Mom Has Cancer*. Abby saw her looking at it and came over and told her that, more than anything, it was a beautiful testimony to living life fully; it was a very comforting book. Last night Maddy wanted to know if Iris agreed it would be comforting to children to know their mom had cancer and Iris said yes, she did think so. Privately, though, Iris was thinking, *What do I know? I never had children. I only wanted them.*

"Do you have some twine we could borrow?" Link asks now.

Iris pulls out the kitchen table drawer where she keeps her red-and-white bakery twine and scissors, and cuts him a long length. They should never have stopped putting drawers in kitchen tables; they are so handy!

"Thanks," he says. And then, "Okay, so . . ."

Iris touches his hand. "Link, I just want to say that I know some hard things are going on in your house right now. I want to tell you that if I can help in any way, anytime, I'd be glad to."

He shrugs. "It's not so bad. And it will be over soon. And then things will be different but mostly back to normal. I don't need so much of my mom's attention anymore."

"Oh!" Iris says. "Right."

He rises up out of his chair. "Coming, Nola?" The girl races out the door behind him.

"Whoa," Maddy says.

Iris looks at her, eyes wide. "I know. I'm . . . I don't know what I am! Are you okay with Nola being in the middle of all this?"

"I think so. I've always gone by how Nola behaves and what she says to gauge how she feels. I try not to second-guess her. And she seems perfectly happy, doesn't she?"

"Absolutely."

"So I guess I'll just leave things alone. I think Abby will let us know when there's something we need to worry about. Oh, I forgot to tell you! Can you pick Nola up at school tomorrow afternoon? I'm driving to a gallery in St. Louis in the morning. I didn't want to say anything until I was sure, but they want to talk about giving me a show in the fall."

"That's wonderful!" Iris says. "Congratulations!"

"Thanks." But in Maddy's voice, as well as in Iris's, is a kind of sadness. Across the way, the light goes on in Abby's bedroom and the women turn to it as though it is a beacon.

Surprise!

❦

In the checkout lane at the grocery store, Nola tells her mother, "Whenever I can't decide something, I just stand still and make myself pure blank on the inside, and then I say, 'Now!' and—presto!—I know what I want to do. It's as plain as a hamburger on a plate."

Maddy wrinkles her forehead. "Plain as a hamburger on a plate?"

"Yeah. John says that. Don't you get it? Like, just a *ham*burger on a *plate*." She offers a one-shouldered shrug. "You might not understand. It's a semaphore."

"'Metaphor,' I think you mean to say. And I guess I understand. Especially if the plate is white. And there's nothing but a burger on it. I guess I get it."

In the car on the way over, Maddy told Nola in as light a voice as she could muster that she was trying to decide if it might make more sense for them to live permanently here, in Mason, rather than in New York. "You do like

Mason, don't you?" Maddy asked, and Nola said, "Yes! I already told you about six hundred times! *You* want to stay here, right?"

Maddy nodded. "I do."

"Well, me, too. So"—Nola dusted off her hands—"all done. We stay here."

Now Nola says, "I can't wait to see the baby."

"What baby?"

"You know. Link's mom is going to have a baby and it might be here by Halloween and Link says it can go trick-or-treating with him because everybody loves babies. People will get all goo-goo-gah-gah and they'll give him more candy than usual. But I get all the Starbursts because Link hates Starbursts."

"Wait. Abby is going to have a baby?"

"Yes! You didn't know? And she just found out it's a girl, like the ring said! Remember when we put Abby's wedding ring on that twine you gave us and it moved around in a circle? That means it's a girl. Didn't I tell you?"

"No!" Maddy rewinds events in her mind, begins to see things differently. Correctly. Wait till she tells Iris. A baby!

Nola starts unloading the cart onto the conveyor belt. "Oh. Well, hee-hee, now you know. I thought you knew about the baby! I heard you and Iris talking about helping to take Abby to the doctor."

"When?"

"Ho, I hear *lots* of things you say—don't worry."

This remark sends Maddy's brain into a kind of frantic hide-and-seek with itself, trying to remember if there is other sensitive information Nola might have been privy to. Nothing she can recall.

A few days ago, Iris told Maddy that Monica Dawson had come to Abby's house to pick her up for a doctor's appointment. "Maybe we ought to offer to drive Abby to her appointments, too," Iris said. "Jason is busy trying to hold down the bookstore, and Monica's making a pretty big sacrifice, taking time away from the Henhouse."

"Sure," Maddy said. "But I don't think Monica minds. The people in this town don't look at it that way. You help your neighbor, here. Period."

It was true. People left bouquets of flowers on doorsteps, paper bags of tomatoes. If you were the first one out after a snowfall, you shoveled your neighbor's walk as well as your own.

Maddy and Iris did offer their driving services, but Abby never took them up on it. Now it occurs to Iris that she and Monica are probably both going to the same OB practice.

"I'm so happy about this news," she tells Nola. "Let's go over to Baby Love and get Abby a little gift."

"What?"

"I don't know. Maybe a pretty maternity top?"

"Okay."

Nola snatches a bag of potato chips before it is bagged,

then attempts to bat her eyelashes. It looks like Morse code. "Can I have some?"

"At home."

"Why?"

"I don't want you to fill up on chips."

"Why not? They're good for you. They are made from vegetables."

"No."

"I will only have *six* chips."

"No."

"Four?"

Maddy gives Nola a *That's enough* look.

Nola drops the chip bag. Then, while Maddy signs the credit card receipt for the groceries, Nola leans on the handle of the cart, moving it back and forth in irritating little jerks.

"When we get home, I want you to go outside and run around for a while," Maddy tells her. "Good grief."

"Can't."

"Why not?"

"I need to keep a lookout for Matthew."

Maddy freezes. "What do you mean? Is he coming?"

Nola sighs. "Sheesh. You don't know that, either?"

That night, while Iris pores over cookbooks, Maddy comes to sit with her. "So I've got news."

"What?"

"First of all, guess who's pregnant?"

Iris looks up. "Oh, my God. You?"

"Nope. Abby."

"*Abby?*"

"Yup."

Iris closes the cookbook she's been looking at. "When did she tell you?"

"She didn't. Nola did."

"Why didn't Abby tell us?"

Maddy shrugs. "Maybe she assumed we knew, since the kids did. Or she might have wanted to wait a while to talk much more about it, just to make sure everything was okay. A lot of people don't tell anyone until they're past the first trimester."

"Well, *this* puts a whole different spin on things!" Iris says. "What good news!"

"I know." Maddy laughs.

"And here I was, thinking the worst!" Iris says.

"Me, too. But then that's kind of a habit of mine."

"But the kids knew."

"The kids knew. And here's even bigger news: Guess what else Nola told me?"

"What?"

"Matthew's coming."

"He is?"

"Yup."

"When?" Iris asks.

"Don't know. He's on the way."

"Wow."

"Right?"

"Are you glad?" Iris asks.

"We'll see," Maddy says.

A Visitor

Iris is sitting at the kitchen table with her computer, writing copy for her baking classes. When she has finished, she checks her email, scrolling quickly through the many messages, deleting several of them without opening them. She remembers when she first got email, a friend of hers saying, "You'll love it!" She didn't love it then and she doesn't love it now. She appreciates the practical aspects, but it seems to her that email has mostly just aided and abetted the slow death of real communication. She won't use emojis as a matter of principle. At least the junk emails don't waste paper. But they certainly make you wonder how these people get addresses. Using the computer is becoming less a convenience for her than an exercise in time-wasting and paranoia.

She feels too young to be so crankily dug in, but the more time she spends on a computer, the less connected to real life she feels. That's one of the reasons she likes to visit John at the farm. Something about being there makes her feel so relaxed, so connected in a fundamental way to the things that matter most to her.

Unbenownst to him, she submitted a full-price offer on the place last week. She went to Rhonda House's office ("Mason's Make-It-Happen Realtor!"), and after Rhonda asked her a million times if she wouldn't rather look at cute little houses like this one and that one and *Oh, hey, what about* that *one*, she helped Iris fill out the necessary paperwork, and the owners accepted immediately. She'll offer to rent the farm to John for whatever he can afford, plus his help in fixing the place up. Already she has ideas for the kitchen, including a stone fireplace, and a bedroom that faces east, for the sunrises. She wants to enlarge the garden, and the idea of acquiring a lot of animals— even some llamas and goats!—holds great appeal. Some chickens, too—why not? Iris wonders how many other people who were forbidden to have pets as children (Iris's mother: *That's what zoos are for*) go overboard later on in life. But John could help her; she thinks he might like it a lot. He had told her that coming from a farm himself, his father had taught him a lot about land and animals—his father did like animals; that was one good thing about him, John said. He could whittle, he carved beautiful birds from willow wood. He was quite good-looking, and he had a beautiful tenor voice like Gordon MacCrae, too. He told Iris he figured that's why his mother fell for his father: *Sure, her own Gordie MacCrae, isn't it, carrying her across the threshold all fine and romantic*. That was about it for his father's good qualities, though. Mostly he had a wildly unpredictable and violent temper that got triggered by anything from the weather to a T-shirt not whitened to his liking. Once, when the phone rang during dinner, he flung his plate across the kitchen. Iris gasped when John told her this; he laughed.

Considering the life John has had, Iris finds it no surprise that he likes the peace of being in the out-of-doors. And a farmhouse is as close as you can get to still being outside when you're in. She thinks maybe, in time, they could be happy living there together. She could teach her classes from there as well as she does from the house she's in now. And what fun for people to go out to the henhouse and gather the eggs they'd need for that day's recipes!

She is just about to delete an email from yet another address she doesn't recognize when she realizes she does recognize it. It's a new email address, but her ex-husband's name, Ed, is in it. His message is brief but it makes her slam the lid of her computer down and stare straight ahead:

Iris. Divorced again. And just wondering. Any chance we could meet? Anytime. Anywhere.

The doorbell rings, and for one panicked moment she thinks it's Ed, who did not often wait for her answer to a question he'd asked her before forging full speed ahead on his own. He'd call her at her shop and leave a message asking if she'd like to see a play that night. By the time she called him back, he'd have gotten tickets. One Christmas, when he asked about going to Paris for the holiday, she said, "Huh. *May*be."

"Good," he said, and showed her two first-class tickets on Air France.

She goes to the door, full of trepidation. But the person standing on the porch is not Ed. "Matthew!" she says.

"How are you, Iris?" He's oddly formal. Scared-looking, Iris thinks.

She motions him in. "Maddy and Nola are at the grocery store. They'll be back any minute. Come in! How nice to see you! Would you like some coffee?"

Matthew sits stiffly in the kitchen with Iris, making idle chitchat while she prepares coffee, and then, after she puts his cup before him, he takes hold of her wrist. "Iris, please tell me. What's going on with Maddy?"

"Well, I . . . I don't really think I'm the one to answer that, Matthew. When Maddy comes back, why don't the two of you go out and talk, and I'll take care of Nola?"

"But has she—"

He stops talking as the front door opens.

"Hey, Iris?" Maddy calls. "Can you help carry bags in? I'm afraid we got way more than we planned on."

Matthew goes out into the hall. "Why don't I do that?" he says.

"Yay, you're here!" Nola says, and runs to him.

Maddy leans against the wall. "Hi, Matthew." She looks over at Iris, standing behind him. Iris shrugs. *Don't ask me!*

Maddy and Matthew have gone out to dinner, and Nola has asked to take her bath unsupervised in any way, saying that she wants to practice her singing for the talent show at school tomorrow, plus she knows how to swim, plus she is too old to be hovered over by a human drone, so Iris goes into her room to read. But she can't pay attention to the words on the pages, and so she closes the book and puts it back on the shelf. How unsettling to hear from Ed. She has no idea how to respond to him. She supposes she owes it to him to at least see what he might want to talk about. But what if he wants to get back together? She has no interest in that at all. It would be true even if she weren't in love with another man. And, like it or not, she is in love with John. Like it or not, she has never felt about anyone what she feels for him, and part of the reason is his extreme differentness.

When she abruptly revealed her feelings for John at Confession Club, and revealed as well a kind of shame at feeling this way about a homeless man, Joanie said, "Did you ever hear that Elaine May quote 'The only safe thing is to take a chance'?"

"No," Iris said, wondering if that could possibly be true.

"Well, I'll tell you a story," Joanie said. "I was a real

Goody Two-shoes in high school. But one night my three best girlfriends and I decided to walk on the wild side. There was this club we'd all heard about right up against the tracks, it was called The Yard Dog, and the bad kids went there, the greasers and the girls who rolled up their skirts and peroxided their hair and put out. Everybody said they did dirty dancing at that club, and we wanted to see. It was supposedly real dirty. We'd heard that when they were dancing, boys would pick up girls and turn them upside down, so that their faces would be right in . . . well, you know. We'd heard there was drinking there, too, and it didn't matter if you were underage—they never carded anybody. I had never had a drink.

"We figured we'd have a great time there because we were all pretty cute." She looks down at her gut. "I was cute then! I didn't have all this blubber. I don't know how I got all this blubber. Well, yes I do, but never mind.

"Anyway, we got to the club and pulled into the parking lot and then we all got real quiet. There were motorcycles everywhere. There were a bunch of guys wearing black leather jackets grouped around the entrance, smoking and drinking beer and laughing real loud. I was scared but I was mostly excited, and I said, 'Well, we've come this far—let's go in!' Emily Smitch made us wait while she wrote her name and address on a gum wrapper and stuck it in her bra so that if she got robbed and killed, someone would know how to reach her family.

"We went in, and the place reeked of beer and there

was so much smoke in the air. It was crowded on the dance floor, and the kids were all pressed up against one another and grinding away. We didn't quite get what they were simulating, but I thought it was so interesting to watch. And they did that upside-down thing, too, and some of the girls' skirts flew over their heads and nobody cared except us, standing there holding on to one another with our eyes wide, all of us dressed in our little flowered Villager blouses and A-line skirts and charm bracelets. A boy came over to ask me to dance and I said, 'No thank you, but I would like a sloe gin fizz.' 'A *what?*' he said, and I told him again and he just flipped me off and went to ask someone else to dance.

"We stayed only a little while longer. One of the girls had to pee but she was afraid to go in the bathroom. So we left; we had decided to go to Steak 'n Shake like we usually did. Just after we'd gotten back in the car, a guy came screeching into the parking lot, and he made those other greasers look like altar boys. All the wrong things, as I saw it then: hair slicked back, a car that was just a wreck—pea green, and he'd painted all these things on it. 'Vomit' that was one. Now, why would you ever want to write 'Vomit' on your car? In bright yellow? He pulled in next to us and revved up his engine real loud before he cut it. We were all looking at him, and the other girls were absolutely horrified when he got out of his car and stood there with his hands on his hips, checking us all out in a kind of squinty-eyed way. I could see that everyone else was petrified, but I was fascinated.

"He was completely the opposite of the boys we usually went for, the ones from the private school the next town over. Those boys had Beatle cuts and wore madras shirts with status hooks and Weejuns with no socks. They drove GTOs and Mustang convertibles and some of them even had 'Vettes. This guy wore a white T-shirt and black jeans and dirty boots with chains on them and there was a toothpick hanging out the side of his mouth. But there was something about him. I was attracted to him.

"He came over to our car, where I was riding shotgun, and he leaned in the window and looked at all of us and then he pointed at me and said, 'Yeah. You. Sheila. Come here for a minute and sit in my car with me. I want to talk to you.'

"'My name isn't Sheila,' I said, and he said, 'It is now.' He opened the car door and stood back. And despite the fact that my girlfriends were squealing like little pigs and telling me not to go—in fact, Lindy Miller, who was the head cheerleader, was screaming, 'CALL-THE-COPS! CALL-THE-COPS! CALL-THE-COPS!'—in spite of that, I went over and got in his car. He had a six-pack on the floor, and he asked me if I wanted one. I said no, and he nodded and said, 'I'm not surprised.' And then he just looked at me and said, 'Give me a kiss, baby.' And I did it! And let me tell you something, that guy was some kind of kisser. After that, he said, 'I know what you think of me. But would you go to a concert with me tomorrow night?'

"'Who's playing?' I asked.

"'James Brown,' he said, and I like to flat-out died. I loved James Brown, I still do, I had his record on just the other day when I was cleaning the downstairs powder room. It was the *Live at the Apollo* album, where the MC introduces James by saying, 'The *hard*est-working man in show business, the amazing Mr. *Please Please* himself!'

"Anyway, I told my parents I was going to a concert in St. Louis—they probably thought James Brown was a classical pianist—and that boy and I drove all the way to the city, and there James was up on the stage, sweating bullets, falling to his knees and having someone come out and throw a cape over his shoulders and pretend to beg him to get off the stage before he killed himself, but no, he'd get up and fling off his cape and belt out another one. He did that again and again. And the place would just erupt every time, girls screaming so loud you thought your eardrums would burst. The drama at a James Brown concert—*If you leave me, I'll go crazy*—beats the hell out of all the pyrotechnics and flying around on wires and wearing meat dresses like they do now, I'll tell you that. His kind of drama got right into your twiddle-dee-dee."

"James Brown beat his wives," Rosemary said.

"Rosemary," Joanie said tiredly.

"What? He did!"

"Yes, he did. But that is not the part of James Brown I'm talking about now. Okay?"

"Fine," Rosemary said, and crossed her arms, which, as they all knew, meant she wouldn't talk much or at all for the rest of the night.

Joanie went on. "That boy I went to the concert with, his name was Raleigh, and he was dressed up so nice when he picked me up, tie and Canoe cologne and everything, and he took me out for some dinner before the concert. It was just a greasy spoon, but it was good. We had fried shrimp, I remember, and it was real good. When he paid the bill, he left the tip in coins, including pennies, and I had the feeling that this date had just wiped him out, that he had used up all the money he had.

"He was real nice the whole time, and the concert was great, and after it was over, we went to the river and he spread his jacket out for me and we sat on the banks and just talked. His father worked construction; his mom had died when he was four. He had gotten drafted, he was leaving for basic training in a week, and he said he didn't mind, it was his duty, he just hoped he didn't get greased and come home in a body bag. He looked over at me and he said, 'So, Sheila . . . ' and he laid me down so gently in the grass and just kissed me and not once did he try to feel me up. And since this is Confession Club, I will confess that I actually wanted him to. I'm telling you, girls, I wanted him to do *everything* to me. For the first time in my life, I was kind of sticking my boobs up like *Woo-hoo, come and get it!* and I was writhing around like a *serpent*—oh, my girlfriends would have called me such a slut. But when he kissed me like that, I couldn't help it; I felt out of control. Actually, now that I think of it, I'll bet that concert may have had something to do with it.

"But you know what? That boy did not touch anything but the side of my face and my neck, and it was so gentle, how he touched me. On the way home, realizing how close I had come to going all the way, I thanked him. I said, 'Thanks for not taking advantage of me,' and he laughed and said if he wanted that, he sure enough knew where to get it. And I got jealous! I got jealous of whoever it was who would do things like that with him. When he dropped me off, he asked if we could go out again the next night and I said, 'Yes, pick me up at seven.' But my parents were waiting up for me and they gave me the third degree and then said I couldn't go out with him again. 'But why?' I said. 'Because of his car? That's just a joke!' But my dad stood up and said, 'You'll not go out with him again,' and left the room, and that was that.

"He came the next night and he rang the doorbell and I had to pretend I wasn't home. I looked out my bedroom window and there he was, standing on the front porch, his hands in his pockets. He rang the doorbell one more time and then he just walked away and got back in his car and drove off, very quietly."

"Wow," Gretchen said. "You never told me that story. So 'Leader of the Pack.'"

"It was!" Joanie said. "And I never felt the way I did for him for anyone. I still wonder sometimes what would have happened between the two of us if I'd followed my heart. He was not like anyone I'd ever met, and I just liked him so *much*. I wonder how he turned out. I wonder how all those wild kids turned out. I'll bet they were fun to hang out with. Oh, I know some of them came to no good and there were always rumors about how the nasty girls ended up in homes for unwed mothers. But I'll bet a lot of those kids turned out to be real creative—artists, maybe. But mostly I just still think a lot about how *he* might have turned out. I'd google him, but I never even learned his last name. Just his first name. Raleigh."

Joanie laughed. "You know, after my divorce, I used to fantasize that he'd come into the library someday, and he'd be older, but I'd recognize him right away. And he'd walk up to me sitting there at the checkout desk, and there would be a line of people waiting—more romantic if there was a line—and when it was his turn, he'd say, 'Hello, Sheila. Remember me? I'd like to check you out and take you home and keep renewing you.' Wouldn't that have been clever?

"Oh, shoot, now I'll probably dream of him tonight and whenever I dream of him I wake up so sad and lost-feeling." She sighed. "He's just this *memory*, you know, this kind of encapsulated, sort of . . . emerald-green memory, of the road not taken." She took a big drink of wine, and the table was silent for a while, until Rosemary deigned to speak, asking, "What do you mean, 'emerald-green'?"

"For Christ's sake, Rosemary, it's *poetry*," Dodie said.

"Well, I think she's mixing metaphors or something," Rosemary said, and then Dodie heaved herself up and held her wineglass over Rosemary's head, tipping it dangerously.

"Go on and do it—I dare you," Rosemary said. "I need to wash my hair anyway. And then you can pay your fine to the Whoops! jar."

From downstairs, Iris hears Maddy and Matthew come in. They're speaking quietly. It would probably be nice if she gave them some space.

She calls John, who answers his phone sounding out of breath. "Hey," she says. "Would you like some company?"

There is a long pause, and just when she's ready to reneg, he says, "Sure," and it sounds like he's smiling. Or maybe she just wants him to sound that way. In any case, she's going. She changes clothes, puts on some lipstick, runs a brush through her hair.

On her way out, Iris sees Maddy in the kitchen, standing in front of the open refrigerator. Matthew is in the living room, sitting in an armchair with his head back, his eyes closed, smiling.

"I thought I'd go out and see John for a while," Iris says. "I'll be back late, or maybe tomorrow morning, in plenty of time to set up for class."

Maddy turns around. "Okay."

Her voice sounds like she has a cold, and her eyes are red.

"Are you okay?" Iris whispers.

Maddy moves closer. "Matthew told me that when Nola was on Link's phone with him the other day, she asked if he'd like to move back here, because she and I both wanted to live here again. Guess what he said? He said, 'Of course.' That simple. I never even asked him. I was afraid to ask him. I just assumed he wouldn't want to be back here. But it turns out he loved living here, he just moved to New York for me, so my photography would have a better chance to get noticed. So we're staying. I don't know why I can't stop crying. Too much good news lately, I guess. Bad news I can handle. I expect bad news. I've dealt with bad news all my life. Good news makes me cry."

She laughs. "I'm getting as sentimental as Arthur was; maybe it's from being in his house again. What a lovely old softy he was. He'd tear up over the littlest things. Right after Nola was born, he was so weak, but he used to rally enough to hold her a little. He'd run his finger down her cheek so gently and he'd tear up and have to blow his nose after he gave her back to me. But then he was so strong about the hard things, so measured and calm. I never met a man so completely comfortable and open with his feelings. I wish he'd have been my father. I guess he did become my grandfather. I think I came back to Mason in part because I feel closer to him here. Sometimes I go out to his grave and talk to him. I sit with my back against his headstone and I feel . . . I don't know. Home." She shrugs. "Anyway, I'm here for good!"

Iris hugs her. "I'm glad for you, Maddy." And she is glad. She's also thinking, *Uh-oh. I'm going to have to move.* She'll tell John about buying the farm tonight. She'll get things going. In the car, she fashions her hair into a loose braid; she thinks he might like it that way.

Jiminy Cricket

⚜

After Iris calls, John lights the big candle on the kitchen table. He straightens the few supplies he keeps on the kitchen counter. He opens the window, then closes it. Then opens it. Then he sits waiting, but his knee won't stop jumping up and down, so he goes outside.

It's a glorious night: a clear sky, no clouds, the stars out in abundance. It's neither warm nor cold, it's that perfect temperature for . . . well, for anything. He lies on his back, his hands behind his head. Since he saw the photo of Laura, he can't get her out of his mind. He's never been one to go back to anyone or anything, but now he feels he must. He has a wish for something he can hardly admit to himself.

Up above is a glowing body so clear and bright that, at first, he thinks it's an airplane. But no, it's not moving; it's probably Venus or Jupiter. He stares at it, and the memory of watching *Pinocchio* comes to him, the scene where the cricket sits on the windowsill and sings, *When you wish upon a star* . . . His mother had taken him into town to see the movie one cold and rainy day, and since the weather was so bad, they'd decided to watch the movie twice. What was he, six? Seven? They'd had popcorn for dinner, and his mother had said, "Won't your father be jealous, though?" His father had not been jealous, he'd been angry about coming home to a note on the kitchen table in place of a hot dinner. When they got back, John watched his mother move quickly past his glowering father, who was sitting at the kitchen table with his paring knife and blood sausage and beer. She said not one word to him, she only went upstairs and drew a bath, and John sat outside the door to try to protect her, though he knew quite well the odds against his being able to do that. But that night, his father left her alone, and John thought it was because he had wished on a star on their way home, asking for his father to be nice to his mother. If it worked for a cricket, he'd reasoned, why wouldn't it work for him? And then, apparently, it did. His mother emerged from her bath smelling of rose oil, her one indulgence. She kissed John and sent him to bed and then went to bed herself, and when his father joined her, John listened carefully but there was nothing but low chatter, friendly chatter, then the sound of the springs creaking from someone turning over, and then: nothing. Quiet. And John had wept with relief, though he'd regretted being such a baby.

Now he regards the bright star above him and sings softly, "*When you wish upon a star / Makes no difference who you are."* It makes for a sudden ache in his chest; it is a revelation, the idea that somewhere it *doesn't* matter who you are. Or were. And he makes a wish upon a star again, for the first time since that night when he was a little boy.

He hears a car pull in, and he rises to his feet to begin walking back to the house. It will take a while; he's walked out farther than he ever has before, past the hollowed-out oak where the owls congregate, past the stand of wild blueberries, darkening now, but not at the point where if you touch them, they fall into your hand—that's the time to gather them, when there's no resistance at all. That's when they're ready.

He quickens his pace; he doesn't want Iris to think he's not here. Though he won't be here for much longer. He knows where Laura lives, thanks to the Internet. He knows she's retired from being a nurse. He knows she volunteers at the VA. He knows she has an old yellow Lab named Preacher. He believes that if he shows up, she won't slam the door in his face. Thinking of that, knocking at her door, makes his knees nearly buckle beneath him. Him knocking, her opening the door, staring blankly at him at first, then saying only, "John."

When he gets to the house, he sees Iris in the kitchen with her back to him, sitting straight and still in the chair, her hands folded on the table. She is wearing blue jeans and sandals and a white off-the-shoulder blouse with red and blue embroidery, birds and flowers. She is such a beautiful woman, but that's not what John finds best about her. He loves that she is so kind, that she is a straight shooter, that she laughs in bed. She is the kind of woman who gives freely, without entering a mark on her side of the ledger. And isn't it heaven, those desserts she makes, isn't it a poor man's heaven.

When he comes in the door, he can tell she hasn't heard him. He walks up behind her and puts his hand on her shoulder. And without turning around, she puts her hand over his.

"I shouldn't have done that," he says. "I might have scared you."

"I know you by your hands," she says.

She turns to face him and smiles.

He kneels before her. Kisses her hand. Lays his head in her lap and closes his eyes. "Iris," he says, and she says, "I have something to tell you."

The Value of Pie

After teaching her Creative Birthday Cakes class, Iris climbs the stairs slowly to her bedroom. A *nap*, she's thinking, before she heads over to Rhonda House's office later this afternoon for the closing on the farmhouse. She had expected this day to be so joyful; now it's not. She still wants the place, but living there isn't going to be quite what she thought it was.

Last night, she had a look at John's journal. She knew it was wrong, but while she was waiting for him, an ominous feeling suddenly came over her. Never mind her deep feelings for John, what did she know about him, really? And there was his journal, which might tell her something she needed to know.

She went to the window by the door to see if she could see him coming; there was still a bit of light. She figured he'd gone out into the fields to get a bouquet of fresh wild-flowers. The stems of the ones he had out on the table now were bent over the edge of the jar, and pink and white petals dotted the table. She went to the other window: no sign of him. She sat back down, picked up the journal, and turned to the most recent entry, dated today, written with a fountain pen in beautiful script:

On a night when I need to prepare myself for leaving tomorrow, Iris calls. I'd been remembering Laura in a way I have not permitted myself to do for so long: I saw her on our wedding day. I saw her weeping in my arms after a sad movie, singing Joan Baez songs to me while she played her beat-up guitar, making dinner in a way that always looked like making art. I remembered how we read to each other, how we relished our early-morning walks, I remembered my hand on the swell of her belly where our child grew inside her, I remembered our son's outraged entrance into the world, Laura quieting him with a touch and a murmur. My fear at seeing her again is matched by my need; I am at war with myself.

But then there is Iris on the phone, her voice a lasso, and my thoughts of Laura disappear and I say yes to Iris coming; yes, I say, come ahead.

What came next was:

INVITING A FRIEND TO SUPPER
by Ben Jonson

But, at our parting we will be as when
We innocently met. No simple word
That shall be uttered at our mirthful board,
Shall make us sad next morning or affright
The liberty that we'll enjoy tonight.

Those lines were his goodbye to her.

She closed the journal and put it back exactly as it had been. Her chest ached; she could scarcely breathe. She clasped her hands upon the table, and waited. And then he was there, his warm hand on her shoulder, and then his handsome head in her lap. And when he said her name, she told him that she'd heard from her ex-husband. He lifted his head and looked up at her and said what a coincidence; he was headed out tomorrow to go and knock on the door of his ex-wife. His face was twisted with feeling. And she made it easy for him. She told him it was good he was going, of course he should go, she was glad he was going, safe travels. She kissed his mouth, which was beautiful, all of him was beautiful, and she went out the door. On the way home, she turned off the radio and rolled down the window to feel the night air and to hear the night sounds. She loosened her braid and let her hair blow free. Just before coming into town, she pulled over to the side of the road and got out of the car. She walked out into a fallow field and lay down and appealed to the stars, which offered nothing but a dome of dispassionate beauty. It occurred to her to weep. Instead she went home and put her stained peasant blouse in the sink to soak. Everything came off; she'd caught it in time.

Now she lies on her bed and closes her eyes, but she can't sleep. She's thinking of the email Ed sent her. Maybe she should see him. Maybe he'd like to come to see this town she's moved to. Or maybe she'd like to go back to Boston. Maybe it's not too late to adopt a child with Ed. That was why their marriage failed, after all; and she knows that he now understands why she wanted a child.

She gets up and goes to her computer.

Ed. What a surprise to hear from you. And a surprise, too, to hear that you're divorced again. I know enough about divorce to know that no one who goes through it emerges unscathed, and I truly hope for the best for you, your former wife, and your child. What else can one say under these circumstances? Perhaps that I wonder how and why it all came about.

You ask about our getting together.

She sits thinking, the cursor blinking. In her mind's eye, she sees Ed at the kitchen table in his blue plaid flannel pajamas and handsome tortoiseshell glasses and the slippers she got for him from L.L.Bean. He's reading stories to her from *The New York Times* and *The Boston Globe* as she makes them stuffed French toast, and she is finding comfort in their shared outrage over the stupidity and cowardice of politicians. He's inside her, moving slowly, pushing her hair back from her face, telling her she's beautiful. He's opening the car door for her, he's presenting her with a triple-scoop cone from Park Street Ice Cream in Natick square, he's yelling "Oh, come *on!*" at the Red Sox. He's holding her hand as they sit in the courtyard of the Isabella Stewart Gardner Museum; they're browsing for books at the Harvard Coop; they're sharing a cannoli at Mike's Pastry after dinner at Giacomo's in the North End; they're driving up to Rockport for some new watercolors; they're visiting the Arnold Arboretum on Lilac Sunday, listening to the BSO play in the midst of the hickory trees.

She closes her eyes, rubs her forehead. Then she grabs her car keys and goes over to the Henhouse.

When she arrives, she sits at the counter, the station where Monica is working these days—less running around for a woman as pregnant as she, and she escapes sitting all the time, as she must do when she's the cashier. When Monica sees Iris, she comes over with a cup of coffee. She puts the coffee in front of Iris and says, "What can I do you for? After I bring it to you, I'll sit with you."

"Got any crumb-topped cherry pie?"

"Sure. Do you want it à la mode?"

"I want it double à la mode."

"Be right back."

Monica returns with a huge slice of pie covered with ice cream. Iris says, "Do you have Boston cream pie today, too?"

"Yeah, we've got that. You want to switch?"

"Nope, I want both," Iris says.

Monica hesitates just a moment, then brings out the Boston cream pie. She sets it before Iris and says, "I've done that. Can't decide, so I get them both. I always tell myself I'll just eat half of each, but nope, I eat everything. Sometimes I'm just in the mood to do that. And Tiny—well, he's always in the mood to do that."

"But he's losing weight," Iris says. "I saw him the other day and his face looks so much thinner."

Monica moves from behind the counter and sits on the stool beside Iris. She drinks from a huge tumbler of water she brought out from the kitchen with her. "Yup, we are the water-drinking champions of the world. I do it to keep hydrated; he does it as part of his diet. He wants to be in shape for the baby. I told him, 'Hon, you get up with him at night and you'll lose weight all right. 'Fact, just get up with him every time he cries—how about that?' And you know Tiny. He said it would be his pleasure. He said it would be his honor. Oh, that man is so in love and he hasn't even laid eyes on that baby in the flesh, he just sits staring at the ultrasound photos for what seems like hours. Isn't it a miracle, Iris, the things a baby can do?"

Iris nods. Swallows. Then she says, "Could I also get a side of mashed potatoes and gravy?"

"Lord," Monica says. "This must be man trouble. Is it man trouble?"

Iris nods again, staring into her plate.

"Come back in the kitchen with me," Monica says.

"That's okay," Iris says. "You're busy."

"Not at the moment. And hey. I own the joint." She lines up Iris's dishes on her arm. "Come on."

Telling It Like It Is

❧

Back at home, Iris returns to the keyboard. She deletes what she's written to Ed, and begins again.

Dear Ed,

I think it must be a fantasy many people might have, that of getting back together with their ex-spouse. I confess that since reading your email, I have been thinking about our doing that, even though you did not mention it specifically as something you would like to do. But in case you did have it in mind when you wrote to me, I'd like to tell you what I think of the idea.

I believe we had a good marriage, one that became derailed over our disagreement about whether or not to have children, our waiting, and then my being unable to have them after that awful infection. If we were to revisit the idea of adopting a child together, could we get back on track? I don't know, but I'm sorry to say I think not.

I teach baking classes in this town (I can imagine your eyes widening), and sometimes the classes are for children. At the last class I had for them, there was a seven-year-old having her birthday that day, and she said, "I'm seven. That's the first old age, right?" I believe she may have been referring to Shakespeare's Seven Ages of Man—who knows how she came across it? At any rate, it made me think about the fact that we do seem to go through a kind of shedding of skins, not only at regular intervals as we age, but because of events and circumstances.

I am no longer the Iris you knew, Ed, and probably you are not the Ed I knew. The changes I've undergone since moving to this small town have been profound, and it would be hard for me to try to articulate them—you've got to be here to see here. I can't imagine ever wanting to live anywhere else, but I can't see the two of us living together in Mason. I don't believe you'd be happy here.

I think it best that we take our final leave of each other, dear Ed—and you are still dear to me. I will never forget the feel of the top of your head, the basso profundo you attempted when you sang in the shower, the immediate attention you paid to home repairs, such a rare and wonderful quality. I know you as a kind and handsome and intelligent man capable of giving and receiving great love. In fact, it occurs to me now that you might have already found another woman and maybe were writing to share that news in case . . . I don't know, maybe you need references? (I hope you're smiling.)

I've gone on too long, here. I've indulged my imagination on all fronts too much. So, I will end by saying that I do now and always wish you the very best, Ed. I carry a miniature you forever in my heart.

Iris

She pushes the send button. Then she puts her hands over her face and rocks back and forth in her chair. She can feel the sting of tears, but she does not let them fall.

At the Henhouse, after Iris told Monica about John leaving, and about her idea of maybe getting back with Ed, Monica put her hand on Iris's arm. She said, "Let me tell you something. I work in the food industry, and here's what I know: if you want fried chicken and the restaurant is out of it, you ain't never in a month of Sundays gonna be happy with the hanger steak. You'll be eating it and the whole time you'll be thinking, 'Dang it, I wish they'd have had that chicken.' Don't settle, Iris. Don't do you or your ex like that. I know you're hurting. But you keep on. Walk toward whatever joy you find. You don't know what's going to happen. And in the meantime, get yourself over to see me and Tiny more often. Come and play cards or watch movies with us. Go about your business in the best way you know how, and love will find you. You know what they say: It's like a butterfly—you do better letting it land on you than trying to capture it." She looked over at Roberto, the short-order cook, who'd had his head bowed a little too fiercely over the grill. "Isn't that right, Roberto?"

The color rose in his face.

"Roberto! You and me! Advice to the lovelorn, right? *Nuestro nombre 'Querida Abby,'* huh?"

"*Correcto!*" he said, and turned to face the women. He smiled, batted his eyelashes, spread the dishtowel he kept tucked in his pants over him like a skirt, and curtsied. "May I help your problem, please?"

Iris takes in a deep breath. She has a lot of work to do. She has a lot of plans for the farm that are still in place. She knows what she wants to grow there, what animals she might like to have—and she wants many animals. She'll have a stable. A henhouse!

She turns back to the computer and googles "baby goats." And she smiles, then laughs out loud. For heaven's sake, look at them; they are the very definition of the word *gambol.* She imagines the children she teaches running out to see them, holding out tufts of grass to feed them. In some of their faces will be exaggerated grimaces of fear mixed with pleasure. Iris will help them not to be afraid; she will tend to the children entrusted to her for the time that they are. There really are so many kinds of love in the world. Monica said that, too, and she was right.

It's Been Good
to Know You

❧

Ollie Futters starts her coffeemaker and then sits at her kitchen table to wait for her first cup. She's normally very cheerful in the morning, but today a sad memory is bothering her.

It's that man, John, the way he just up and took off. In her opinion, a person leaves someone or something that suddenly either because he really wants to go, or, ironically, because he doesn't want to leave at all. He came to her door a few days ago and rang the bell and asked if there was anything he could do for her before he left town later that day.

"I don't have anything to repair right now," Ollie said. "You know I keep on top of things." Then, "Come on in, why don't you? I was just fixing to have lunch. You want a BLT? They got that cooked bacon now, makes it real easy."

He hesitated, then said he'd love one.

After they were seated with their sandwiches and potato

salad and pistachio cupcakes from Sugarbutter, Ollie asked, "Where you going?"

"Cleveland," John said.

"What for?"

"Well, to see my ex-wife, as a matter of fact."

"Why?"

John laughed, and Ollie did, too. "Always too nosy for my own good," she said. "Is that why you wanted to do some work for me? Do you need some money for your travels? I'll just give you some."

"No, no," John said. "I was going to do it for free, to thank you for everything."

Ollie sat thinking. Then she said, "I guess I could go and bust something."

"I do want to thank you," John said. "You've been a good friend to me."

"Well, if I'm a good friend to you, then I hope you won't mind my saying I don't think you should go anywhere. You're a good fit for this town, and, believe me, I don't say that to just anyone."

"Thank you."

"Why *are* you going to see your ex-wife?"

"It's hard to explain." He took another bite of his sandwich. "This is really good."

"Don't try to change the subject, young man."

John leaned back in his chair. "I did some bad things to her. It was many years ago. I was just back from Vietnam and I was . . . well, I guess they call it PTSD now, but then if you were feeling the effects of having been in that war, you were kind of on your own. Oh, you could go over to the VA and ask for help, but . . ."

"Like farting into thunder, huh?" Ollie asked, and wiped delicately at the corner of her mouth.

John smiled. "Something like that. Anyway, I was pretty abusive toward her, and I want to see her again to apologize. And to see where she is in her life, and . . . I don't know. I just have to do it."

"You think she's missing you?" Ollie asked.

"I doubt it."

"You think her life is hard now?"

"I don't know. Seems like you don't think this is such a good idea, though—is that right?"

Ollie looked out the window. "Oh, what do I know. I'm just an old woman who never in her life was married or even serious about a man. I don't know why, to tell you the truth." She turned back to John. "But I guess all my free time let me pay a lot of attention to other couples. And I have seen that a lot of people need to unburden themselves at the cost of hurting someone else. Years ago, I had a good friend practically fall apart when her husband came back to see her to make 'amends.' There she was, all fine in a new relationship, and here he comes, waltzing back into her life, looking real good, all cleaned up, and it just threw her for a loop. He comes in and says, 'I'm sorry,' and that makes him feel really good about himself and then he leaves again and—"

"I might not leave again," John said.

"How many years has it been?" Ollie asked.

"Over forty."

"Lord," Ollie said. "Well, it's not my business, so I'm just going to say be careful, that's all."

"I will."

"You might could weed my garden," Ollie said.

"Yes, ma'am. Soon as I finish my cupcake."

"Lord, you're a handsome one," Ollie said. "I'm going to miss looking at you."

Ollie pours herself a cup of coffee and sits back down at the table. She stares at the empty chair across from her. There he was, sitting right there, and she guesses she didn't say the right thing. She looks out the window and scans the sky. It's going to rain. Isn't that perfect, what with her having an appointment this morning for a cut and curl at Hair You Doing. She gets out her magnifying glass and checks the weather report in the local paper. Rain for the next several days. There goes hanging her intimates out on the line on wash day tomorrow, too. She can't lift sheets up anymore, but she at least likes to get her intimates out there. These little disappointments seem like paper cuts; they can bother you more than the big things do.

A story on the front page of *The Town Crier* catches her eye. Benjamin Putterman called the police about an intruder in his backyard. Turns out it was a duck. This is the fourth time he's called the police in a month, they added.

"Well, for Pete's sake," Ollie mutters. "You don't have to broadcast it."

Poor Benjamin. He's as old as she is, maybe older, and still managing to live alone, though for how much longer, no one knows. He has a nice little house, but he likes best to sit on a lawn chair in his garage, from where he manages Benji's Wondrous Bargains, his version of a pop-up store. He's been doing it for years. He's got wooden shelves built along one side of the garage to display his wares. He keeps hours of his choosing: you know he's open when his sign is out. He sits in his garage in a T-shirt, baggy pants, red suspenders, a Cardinals cap, and house slippers, holding his cigar-box cashbox on his lap, though it is just for his take. He does not make change, as he finds it tiresome. He sells anything he finds interesting, whether it's a potato masher from his house, or an abandoned bird's nest he found outside, or a perfectly good bookshelf he found on the curb, or dahlias in a Dixie cup that he sprouted from seed. His prices are erratic: If he likes you, you can get something for next to nothing. If you're a child, everything *is* for nothing. If he doesn't like you, the cost is basically unaffordable. When Ollie paid eighty-seven cents (the amount that she happened to have in the change compartment of her wallet) for a beautiful, well-seasoned cast-iron pan that had belonged to his mother, he told her about some snoots who had pulled their fancy Lexus right into his driveway the other day so that they could browse his wares. "How much for the cast-iron pan?" the man asked. "Hundred dollars," Benjamin said. The man laughed. "Can you massage the price a bit?" he asked. "Sure," Benjamin said. "How about five hundred dollars?"

Ollie will make Oriental casserole later for the two of them and call Tiny to bring her over to Benjamin's house. He loves it when she surprises him that way, especially when she brings dinner. She won't say anything about the embarrassment of his being on the front page—she knows he will have seen it. Benjamin reads the paper every day, just as she does, and he doesn't even need to use glasses. She won't mention his thinking a duck was a robber, and she won't mention the Depends that she'll bring him because it embarrasses him to buy them. But she'll make sure he's okay, and that he has what he needs, and before she calls Tiny to take her back home, she'll plant a kiss on the top of Benjamin's head. It makes her feel good to help him out. It makes her feel good to help anyone out.

Little Things Mean a Lot

❈

"This is the tricky part," Link tells Nola. "Try not to tear the onion skin. We want to have a big piece to look at."

The two are in Link's room, preparing to use iodine to color the cells of the onion plant so that they can view them under Link's new microscope. It's his favorite possession, and Nola knows she must take extra care in touching it. She feels a tightness in her chest that he is allowing her to do so, and already is thinking of what she might do to reciprocate. Maybe she'll give him the agate she found when she cracked a rock open yesterday. Now, though, she gently peels back the onion skin, using the tweezers Link gave her, and holds up a large piece.

"Impressive," Link says. "I don't think even I could have gotten a piece that big. Here, lay it on the slide. Try to keep it flat." Nola can feel her tongue wanting to come out of her mouth, but she doesn't like to do that in front of people, so she is careful to keep it in. She bends far over the slide, and smooths the skin carefully with the flat end of the tweezers.

"Good," Link says. "Now we put a drop of water on the skin, and then we put a cover slip over it. Watch." He shows her, then says, "Would you like to do the iodine part?"

She nods, tightens her ponytail, and bends to the task.

"Just a little," Link says, his face close to hers. "Just put it on the corner of the cover slip."

"Were you eating butterscotch?" Nola asks.

Link pulls back from her. "Yeah. Don't tell my mom."

"Why?"

"She doesn't like for me to eat candy. But sometimes I do anyway."

"Can I have a piece?"

"Sure. Wait, though." He goes out into the hall for a moment, stands still and listens, then comes back into the bedroom, closing the door behind him. He opens his top bureau drawer and pulls out a sock. "It's in here," he whispers. "Help yourself."

"Wow," Nola says, after she looks in.

"What?" Link asks.

"You have an Atomic FireBall in there, too."

"Yeah. I know. Do you like them?"

"Yeah. A lot. They, like, burn your guts out of your mouth."

"Yeah, it's awesome when it hurts. Sometimes you feel like you need a firehose."

She looks in the sock again, shakes around the candy. "Looks like there's only one FireBall."

"You can have it."

"Thanks!" She unwraps the candy and pops it into her mouth. "Whoa!" she says, almost right away. She has tears in her eyes, but she's grinning.

"Right?" Link says. "Those are really good ones. You get them at Andy's Candies next door to my parents' bookstore. But come over here now. I want to show you what I was talking about."

Nola puts her eye to the microscope. It takes her a while to focus, but then she sees something extraordinary. "There's so much *stuff* in there!" she says.

"It's amazing, isn't it?" Link says. "And see, plant cells have extra things that animal cells don't. They have little things in there called 'chloroplasts' that hold chlorophyll. That's what the plants use to make energy."

Nola shakes her head, still looking into the microscope. "All these *things* are just there, all the time!"

"Right," says Link.

Nola knows that Link has a best friend and it is Hunter Jones, not Nola. But Link is Nola's best friend, all the way. One thing she is very happy about is that they live next door to each other, because they run into each other a lot and oftentimes he just lets her do stuff with him, whatever he's up to at the moment. Yesterday, Link's father helped them build a tire swing in his backyard, and they will both get to use it. But now Link looks at his watch and she knows their time is up.

"I gotta go," he says.

"Okay."

He hesitates, then says, "You're a good kid."

"Oh." She laughs a little, and her hands find each other.

"What are you going to do now?" he asks.

She blows her bangs out of her face. "Whew. Plenty. For one thing, Matthew and I are going with Iris to Tailwaggers. One of Lassie's littermates that got adopted was returned, and they called Iris to see if she wants him. He's going to be Lad. Lad and Lassie, get it? She might get another cat, too."

"Really?"

"Yup."

"I would name a cat Prowler," Link says.

Nola nods. "Good one."

"What time are you guys going?"

"After lunch."

"Can I come?"

She shrugs elaborately. "Sure!"

"Do you want to look in the microscope one more time?" Link asks.

She looks, then pulls back and says, "I just can't believe how different things look under here. Like when you sprinkle sugar on something, you have no idea how it *really* looks."

"Yeah," Link says. "That's one reason I got this microscope."

"Why else?" Nola asks.

Link shrugs. "I don't know if I can explain. I just feel like . . . I look at little things under there, and it seems like they kind of say something about"—he gestures to the window—"out there."

"I know what you mean," Nola says.

"Do you?"

"Yeah. Like I see broccoli sometimes and I think it's like trees."

Link smiles. "Yeah, kind of like that. I look at trees in wintertime, and you know what they remind me of? Nerve cells. And then it makes me think there's like this giant connection of everything to everything. Did you ever see a nerve cell?"

"Nope."

"Next time you come over I'll show you a picture of one," Link says, and Nola grins.

The Way You Are

❖

"It's peaceful here, isn't it?" Maddy asks Matthew. They are out at the cemetery, where Maddy was photographing headstones for a kind of collage she has in mind. Now they are resting against Arthur and Nola Moses's headstones, having a picnic in Arthur's honor.

"I still can't get over the fact that we were married out here," Matthew says, looking over at the tree beneath which they took their vows.

"It was the only place to do it, as far as I was concerned," Maddy says. "If there was anyone I wanted to be at my wedding, it was Arthur. Getting married here meant that he kind of was there. I owe a lot to him."

"I know you do," Matthew says. "I wish I'd known him."

"You would have loved him. Everybody loved him. I guess it was because he loved everyone. But bona-fide, you know? He just *was* love. And his loyalty to his wife, even after she died, was an inspiration."

Matthew crinkles up the wax paper his peanut butter and jelly sandwich was in. "Good sandwich. Thanks."

"Yeah, that was a real gourmet offering."

"It was good!"

Maddy reaches over to wipe away a fleck of peanut butter at the corner of his mouth. "I guess everybody likes PB and J, but I'm going to have to learn to cook, now that Iris is moving out. Actually, I want to learn."

"Me, too," says Matthew. "I got tired of eating out so much the way we did in New York. It will be nice to have a real kitchen. I feel bad about displacing Iris, though. Do you think she's going to be okay, living out there all alone?"

"I think so. At first, she was kind of quiet about it. I guess she was counting on living there with John. But now she seems excited. And she won't be alone. She's got those dogs and cats, and she says she's getting llamas and goats and chickens, too."

"How does she know how to take care of them?"

"She doesn't. But she'll learn. She put a sign up at the feed store for help and she's already hired a couple of girls who are Four-H all-stars. She'll figure it out. She's one of those people who succeeds at every business she tries." Maddy folds up her wax paper and puts it back in the bag. "Want the rest of my lemonade?" she asks, and he nods and drinks it.

"Kinda sour," Maddy says. "I guess I didn't put enough sugar in."

"It was perfect!"

Maddy looks at her watch. "We should go," she says.

Matthew gets up and grabs her hand. "Will you come somewhere with me, first?"

He points with his chin. "Just over to the tree we were married under."

She laughs. "How come?"

He doesn't answer. She goes with him to the tree, to the spot where they stood to commit themselves to each other, and she sees the headstone she was so close to: MARY ANN MAJORS, B. APRIL 12, 1907, D. APRIL 12, 2000. She remembers wondering if it might not be a good idea to die on your birthday.

Matthew takes her hands and looks into her eyes. "Maddy. You have a habit of doubting yourself."

"Tell me something I don't know."

"Okay." He straightens, looks up, then back down at her. "I will never leave you. I will always love you. I will marry you every day from now on for the rest of our lives if you want me to."

"Don't—"

"Maddy, I want you to know that I see you. I see your doubts and your fears. But I see your wondrous side, too. Your kind side. The incredible mother you are to Nola. The way your friends can count on you.

"Look, I'm guessing you haven't told me half of all the terrible things that happened to you when you were growing up. You don't have to tell me all of it, but I want you to know that you can, if you want to. You can't do anything that will make me not want to be with you. I know who I am in love with. I know who I'll stay in love with. You call yourself flighty. Well, good, because I'm Mr. Grounded. Not that I . . . I mean, I'm so glad you wanted to come back here, but if tomorrow you said you wanted to go back to New York City, I'd pack the car."

"I think Nola would have something to say about that," Maddy says.

"No doubt," Matthew says, smiling. "But anywhere you are? To me, that's home."

"Matthew?"

"What?"

She sighs. Scratches her head. Stares off into the distance, then looks back at him. "I just don't know how you can promise such things. There is such uncertainty in all our lives; so much can happen that we never anticipated. And people can have grown in a certain direction that they might never be able to . . . I just don't see how someone can make a commitment like you just did and feel certain that it will last."

"I do," Matthew says. "Love. Trust. Faith. I have enough of all that for both of us. We'll make it. Day by day."

She nods, looks out toward the graves of Arthur and Nola and feels a kind of gentle urging. "Okay," she says finally. She looks up at Matthew. "I'm in."

He laughs.

"I know, that was . . . What I mean to say is . . . What I mean to say is that I love you so much, Matthew. I love you so much! And I don't deserve you, but I'm going to try to. Day by day."

He embraces her, and above them a crow lands in the tree, caws, and takes off again.

"That's good luck, that crow doing that," Matthew says.

"Is it?"

"Has to be. Do you want to go home now and we can try our hand at spaghetti and meatballs?"

She pulls away and looks up at him. "I do."

"Okay," he says, gently. "Let's go."

Leave Well Enough Alone

❦

Just before noon, John is let out in Cleveland from the last ride he got (a good guy, driving a Krispy Kreme truck, and for fifty miles, all they talked about was jazz). He gets a shave and a haircut at a barbershop. At Goodwill, he buys a pair of pants, a shirt, new underwear, and, for five dollars, a pair of barely used sneakers. He brushes his teeth in their men's room, changes into his new clothes, and tosses his old clothes in the trash. The only thing in his backpack now, besides a comb, a toothbrush, and a third of a tube of toothpaste, is his journal, his pen, and his dead phone. In his pocket is the little cash he has left, and the directions to Laura's house that he printed out at the Mason library before he left.

Here and there on the streets of the city he sees homeless men and some women, too. He hands out dollar bills to them whenever they ask. In many of their eyes is a rock-bottomness that John recognizes and remembers. In a small park, he sits on a bench with the hamburger and fries he bought with the last of his cash. He came up short by fifteen cents, and the woman behind him covered him. She reminded him of Iris, not the way she looked, but the way she exuded a kind of calm and kindness. It made his stomach ache, thinking of Iris, and he went to sit on a stool by the window so that he could look at something and be distracted. It's not like him to hold on to things this way; it scares him. And God knows he did Iris a favor to leave; he'd only have messed up her life. That's what he does—he messes things up.

For now, he wants to eat and to think about how he might get to where Laura lives—he can't risk taking the time to hitch there. Even though he is cleaned up, a ride can be pretty hard to come by.

A disheveled man rolls an overloaded shopping cart over to him and sits beside him.

"Excuse me for bothering you," the guy says. "But could you help me out? Just a few dollars, that's all I'm asking. I'm hungry. I haven't eaten for three days. I been on a real losing streak."

"I'm sorry," John says. "I just spent the last of my money. I don't have any more."

The man raises his chin and studies John from under hooded eyes. "Man, one thing I hate is when people lie like that. I know you got money."

"Is that so," John says. "And how is it that you know that?"

The man leans closer to him. His breath smells like liquor; his body odor is in a class by itself. His eyes are bloodshot, his lower lip cracked and caked with old blood. "You got that *air* about you," he says. "You got that air of never suffered, never worried. You set."

John gets up and hands the man his uneaten food. "Take care," he says, and walks out of the park toward the bus stop. He'll ask whatever driver stops first how to get to where he's going—someone at the barbershop said something about senior citizens riding the bus for free. So close now, and this is the hardest part.

After two bus rides and a long walk, John arrives at Laura's address. It's in a gated suburb just outside the city, though an unattended booth by the gate makes you wonder just how secure the place is. John is a little surprised that Laura lives here. He never thought of her as the type who would make a point of keeping people out. But then he never thought of himself as the type who would be homeless, either. By choice. For despite the hardships, it offers something he is loath to give up, part of which is a sense of being plugged into something real. It's kind of like the way so many guys volunteered to go back for more tours to Vietnam: it was awful there, but it was real. Vital.

The lots in Laura's subdivision are all generous sizes, with wooded areas on either side of the houses. He stands behind a tree and watches Laura's house. After a while, he sees a woman walk quickly past a window, and it's her. He's certain. His mouth grows dry; he thinks for a second about leaving. But no.

Just as he's coming out of the woods and headed for her door, he sees a car pull into Laura's drive. A late-model Audi, a nice-looking car, if red. The man knocks on the door and immediately goes in; then he and Laura come outside.

She looks the same. He knows she's aged, but to him she looks the same. The woman who wore braids and long dresses, who eschewed any kind of makeup. The woman whose expression was always one of great peace. A Madonna. Until he nearly killed her. Then she didn't look so peaceful. Then she was full of anguish until the day she got a restraining order, and he imagines that even after that she had some awful days.

Her hair is cut to shoulder length, a blunt and simple style, and it appears that she still doesn't wear makeup. She has on tan slacks and a red blouse, a few gold bracelets on one arm. And look now, the ease with which the man takes her hand, just for the short walk out to the car. Look at how, when the sun gets in her eyes, she only smiles up at him—still that radiant smile. She takes sunglasses out from her purse and puts them on, then says something to the man, a tall, slim guy wearing an Izod shirt and khaki pants, expensive sneakers. Good-looking fellow, if bald. The man says something back, and kisses her.

He can't do it. After all these years, he can't walk up and announce himself to Laura for the purpose of apology. His entire life since he lost her has been an extended apology. She's fine, he sees that, and he sees as well that

that's all he really needed to do, was to see that she is fine. Suddenly, like a door banged open by the wind, startling and declarative, he also knows that he's going to stop walking on his knees in penance now. He's free.

The Audi goes by him, Laura's arm hanging out the window, and for one second he is nearly undone by the desire to touch that arm, browned by the sun, to feel the flesh that he must have caressed thousands of times. He knows the delicacy of the bones in her wrist; he knows the length of each of her fingers. He put a ring on one of those fingers years ago, his heart breaking with joy.

Well. Goodbye, then, Laura. He is without her now and forever. Goodbye.

And so what now? An internal compass recalibrates. He goes out to the road and sticks out his thumb. In California, you don't have to deal with the winter.

The Seventh Commandment

❈

"Biscuit rage, I call it," Gretchen says. "It's that sudden rising up of irrational and completely outsize anger you can experience when you least expect it. You know what I mean: someone takes that last biscuit that you were *just* going to take, and you just want to bite their *ear* off. It's like road rage, only domestic."

Karen says, "That's so funny—my husband just gave a sermon on road rage, and I think it's the first time I saw *everyone* paying attention. But if everyone's ready, I'd like to start."

The women quiet down, and Karen clears her throat. "First, I need to tell you some things about my past. But please remember that it's my past, not who I am now.

"So, as a teenager, maybe fifteen, sixteen, I stole things. And I got away with it. I got away with it every single time, and that just fueled my confidence for doing it the next time. I stole a lot of things. A lot. Maybe for a whole year. Candy, magazines, makeup—"

"I stole some makeup once," Joanie interrupts to say. "It was a sample lipstick so it didn't even come with a top, but I just loved that lipstick. I wore it every single day until it was gone. Caramel Kiss, it was called. And I don't think if I'd have bought it, I would have liked it so much."

"Right," Karen says. "Exactly. Getting away with stealing something makes it better. You use whatever you stole, and each time it's a thrill."

Dodie says, "When I was a teenager and lived in St. Louis, I used to go to the lunch counter at Woolworth's, and one time when the check came, I stuffed it in my purse. But I left a very generous tip. One of the Sydowski sisters taught me that. They were the wild girls in our school, these two girls, Lena and Julie Sydowski, they were called the Sin Sisters, and they were always doing bad stuff. Once I was at the lunch counter when they were there, and I saw them do that and I wanted to try it, too. But it made me feel so awful I never did it again."

"I stole a girdle," Gretchen says. "I put it on and then I just walked right out of the store with it. I was too embarrassed to pay for it because the cashier was my archenemy, and I knew she would tell the whole school that I wore a girdle. And the thing is, I didn't even need one! Not then!"

"My word," says Rosemary, all sniffy and righteous.

"You never stole anything?" Joanie asks.

"I did not."

"*Nothing?*" asks Maddy.

Rosemary sits still, thinking. Then she tightens her

mouth and says, "All right, a Heath bar. Which the check-out girl at the grocery store forgot to ring up and I did not tell her. And, oh! Once I took a roll of toilet paper out of a gas station bathroom. And you know what? I didn't even need it. It was just so tempting. They had so many rolls out, like they were boasting, saying, 'Help yourself—there's lots more where that came from!' And I guess you girls are right—that toilet paper did seem special to me. I put it in the guest washroom, and I felt a little bad when it was gone."

"But, you guys, here's the thing," Karen says. "I was at Gemology yesterday and I stole a *bracelet*." She lifts the sleeve of her blouse. "This is it." She shows the group a gold bangle festooned with tiny diamonds.

Dodie, who is sitting next to her, gasps. Then she says, "Wow, that's *pretty*. Can I try it on?" Karen hands her the bracelet, and Dodie says, "How much was it?"

"Four hundred and fifty dollars," Karen says.

Dodie frowns, turning the bracelet around and around. "Not bad. I would have guessed—"

"What is the *matter* with you?" Rosemary says. "This is not a trunk show! This is grand larceny! Isn't it grand larceny, Toots?"

"I guess it is. It's grand larceny, Karen."

"But I stole it by accident! Or maybe by habit, I guess, because I used to steal jewelry, too—only that was just costume jewelry. Anyway, I was at Gemology the other day picking up a repair, Charlie had fixed Tom's watch. I had to wait because Charlie was showing some guy bracelets, and he was taking forever. After the guy finally picked one out and paid for it, Charlie scooped up the other bracelets and locked them back in the case. When he went in the back to find Tom's watch, I saw something shining on the floor. One of the bracelets had fallen. I picked it up and put it on while I was waiting for Charlie to come back, and then I . . . well, I guess I just forgot or something because I walked out with it."

"Why didn't you just give it back?" Joanie asks.

"Do you know Charlie Zoster?"

"Of course I do. We all do."

"Well, then you know how he is. He mistrusts his own mother. He wouldn't believe that it was a mistake. And that man is a huge gossip. My husband could lose his congregation!"

"Oh, for heaven's sake, I'll bring it back," Toots says.

"But what will you tell him about how you got it?" Karen asks.

"I'll tell him an admirer gave it to me and that something about it seemed suspicious. That's all I'll have to say. He's afraid of me. And besides, he'll just be thrilled to get it back. I might buy it—I sure like it."

"I saw it first," Dodie says.

"Well, then you can buy it," Toots says. "After, you know, it gets returned."

Silence, and then Karen starts to cry. "I'm so embarrassed."

"Have you taken anything else?" Rosemary asks.

"No! Not since high school."

"Then I'd say you're forgiven," Rosemary says. "Now, let's just forget about it and . . . let's just forget about it."

"Forget about what?" Dodie says.

Taking Them Up
on Their Offer

❧

Iris brings corn to pop on the stove when she goes over to Monica and Tiny's house to watch a movie with them. They're going to see *The Shape of Water* again, even though when Monica and Tiny went to see it in the theater, Tiny squirmed the whole time. But he loves his wife, and he loves popcorn you make on the stove, especially with a lot of butter. "I'll endure the movie for the food," he tells Iris when she shows him the jar of Orville Redenbacher popcorn she brought along. She also brought Junior Mints and Good & Plenty and RedVines and Milk Duds and Hot Tamales.

She brought a gift-wrapped onesie for the baby, too, holding back on bringing Monica and Tiny any more of the eight she has bought. So far. She knows Monica's not superstitious about getting things for an unborn baby, because she's told Iris about the things she's bought. But they're short on newborn onesies, she said, so that's what Iris brought tonight. It's powder-blue, with a little lamb embroidered on it, and Iris bought a stuffed-animal lamb to go with it. It was hard for Iris, looking through those baby clothes, knowing she would never buy such things for a baby of her own. But it wasn't as hard as she thought it might be. It helps to know she'll be a sought-after baby-sitter for this little one. Only two and a half weeks to go! When she and Monica saw each other at the Henhouse, Monica's roomy uniform and apron hid the bump well. But now, with Monica dressed in one of Tiny's T-shirts and jeans, Iris can see that she is very close indeed.

"Isn't this the cutest thing," Monica says, unwrapping the onesie. "And oh, Tiny, look! A little lamb to go with it!"

Tiny holds the lamb in his huge hand, and something inside Iris turns a slow somersault. She thinks the most cynical person in the world could still be moved by this kind of love on a father-to-be's face.

Tiny volunteers to pop the corn, and Iris and Monica sit in the living room. Iris makes Monica put her feet up on the hassock; Monica makes Iris share it with her, and throws a quilt over them both.

"How're you doing?" Monica asks quietly.

Iris guesses Monica knows that she misses John. She hasn't talked much about it, but she supposes it's clear to anyone who knows her.

Iris shrugs. "I'm okay. You know how when you lose someone, you keep thinking about all the wonderful things about them, all the good times you had? I'm trying to think about the *bad* times."

"Good idea," Monica says. "Let's talk about that. What were the bad times?"

"Well, there weren't a lot of bad times. That's the problem. I can't think of any. We didn't know each other long enough. He was . . . moody, I'll call it. But there were things just *after* him, he had demons. Still, there was just something about him that I really . . ." She looks over at Monica. "I don't know, is this stupid? I thought we could have had a life together. I hoped the two of us would live on the farm together."

"There's nothing wrong with hoping. Things don't always work out, that's all. But life is funny. You may end up with what you want after all, but in a way that you never expected. Like this movie, right?" She laughs. "I *know* that woman never wished for a *fish* for a lover."

"Until she met him," Iris says. "I have to say, they did make him attractive."

"You really think so?"

"I do," Iris says. "But then I like unusual things."

"Almost done," Tiny yells into the living room.

Monica speaks quickly. "Listen, Iris, I want you to know, that . . . Well, so many people in this town love you, me and Tiny included. I hope you know that."

"Here we go!" Tiny says, coming into the room with a huge bowl of popcorn. Just before they start the movie, he says, "I have made an executive decision. I'm watching until that bathtub scene comes on, and then I'm going out to get my steps in." Tiny tries to walk ten thousand steps a day, and Monica says he gets crabby if he doesn't get them in.

"Okay," Monica and Iris answer together. They're both already fixated on the screen, even though it's only previews now. "I can't wait to see this movie again, I love it so much," Monica says.

"Me, too," says Iris.

"I always love a good romantic movie."

"Did you ever see *Gone with the Wind*?" Iris asks.

"Six times," Monica says, around a mouth full of popcorn.

"You know that scene when Ashley comes home, he's walking down the road, and at first Melanie doesn't know it's him?"

"That's a good scene. She just *runs* to him."

"Wouldn't it be great to have a love like that?" Iris asks.

"I do have a love like that," Monica says, and Tiny beams.

"But I mean, wouldn't you love to *run* to a man you love like that? So romantic!"

"I guess," Monica says. "But I can't run so good anymore. And I doubt Tiny could pick me up now."

Tiny says, "I can still—"

"Shhhhhhh!" both women say, because the previews are over and the movie is starting.

"I can still pick you up," Tiny whispers.

Later, after Tiny has left for his walk and the lovemaking in the film is going on in earnest, Monica says, "Oh, God."

"I know," Iris says softly. "It's so weirdly *sexy*."

"No, it's . . ." Monica stands. "Iris. Iris, I think this is it. I think I'm in labor. I've been having pains all day but Tiny said it was just gas. Why do men always think they know about things they don't know about? This isn't gas. This *hurts*. I think this is it!"

"But . . ." Iris says. "Where's Tiny?"

Monica grabs her phone to call him, and they hear the ringtone in the house.

"He didn't bring his phone! I'm going to kill him!"

"Should I go and look for him?"

"No! Don't leave me alone. Don't leave me alone, Iris."

"Well . . . Shall I take you to the hospital?"

"*Yes*. This is it. I'm sure this is it. Oh, Lord, and I didn't even rinse the supper dishes. They're still in the sink. Let me just—"

"Get in the car," Iris says.

Monica sits down. "Do you think you could bring the car into the living room?" But then she takes in a big breath and gets up and the women walk slowly out to the car.

"*Tiiiiiiiiiny!*" Iris calls, after she seats Monica in her car. "*Tiiiiiiiiiny!*" she tries again. Someone next door opens a window and yells out, "He's out for his *walk*!"

Iris gets into the car, takes a deep breath, and pulls out

onto the street. It's only six blocks. She can afford to go slowly, carefully.

"Oh, Monica," she says. "A brand-new *person* is about to take his place on the earth."

"Yeah," Monica says. "Can we listen to the radio or something?"

An hour later, Tiny comes bursting into Monica's hospital room. "I'm sorry, I'm sorry," he says. He picks up Monica's hand and covers it with kisses.

"The doctor was just in," Monica says. "It won't be long."

"Monica," Tiny says, his voice breaking, and Iris takes this as her cue.

She goes to Monica's bedside and kisses her forehead, squeezes her hand. "You're going to do just fine," she says. "Call me afterward, whenever you can." She hugs Tiny, and goes out into the hall. She leans against the wall, trying to think about what she wants to do. She doesn't want to go home and be with Matthew and Maddy and Nola, another happy family.

She gets into the car and drives out to the farm. Twice now, she has slept in John's old bed, buried under quilts she's brought out there. He cleaned out everything before he left, but not that bed. She wants to wake up on the farm as it was when he was there, and say goodbye to that iteration. This will be her last chance to sleep there as it was when they were there together. Demolition starts tomorrow, and Iris gets to help. Then the carpenter, the plumber, and the electrician are all going to work together to make the place habitable. They've told her she can move in there in six weeks. It doesn't really seem possible, but they assure her it is. She can hardly wait to be living there, with her dogs and all her other animals. She's especially excited about the llamas. Maddy told her that as a spirit animal they symbolize hard work and responsibility and how everything you want can be achieved if you'll just put in the effort every day. She'd read to Iris from something she'd printed out: "'Llamas teach you to persevere because there are always good things waiting for you on the horizon.' See? Right here in black and white." She gave Iris the paper, and Iris folded it up and put it in her pocket. The general contractor she's working with told her that there was a tradition of hiding something in the walls before the drywall goes up—did she have anything she wanted to put in there? Now she does.

Iris herself has learned that llamas are very graceful, curious, intelligent, and gentle. But they're also loners, and they want little care. They remind her of someone she still thinks of with great affection, and supposes she always will.

The Thing That Shall
Not Be Named

❧

"All right, ladies," says Rosemary. "This is it. I'm ready to talk about something very *personal*."

"That's what we do here," says Karen. "Duh."

"Yes, but this is *very* personal."

Silence but for the clink of Toots's fork scraping against her dessert plate. It's only yellow cake and chocolate frosting from the box, but if there's one thing Toots likes, it's yellow cake out of the box. One time, when Confession Club fell on her birthday and the women wanted to gift her with something, she asked for and received a mixing bowl of yellow-cake batter, and she went through a substantial amount of it before asking to have it put in a container to take home.

Rosemary clears her throat. "Okay. For a long time now, Don and I haven't . . . We haven't had sex for *years*. First, things just slowed up, but now everything has stopped altogether. He isn't interested. Doesn't matter how hard I work to keep myself up, he isn't interested.

He's not mean about it, he's just . . . well, he's *nothing*. A couple of times, I've tried to talk to him about it and he says he's sorry, and that he feels bad, but he just has no desire. He sees no point in seeing a doctor—he says it's natural. Then the other day he said right out of the blue, 'And I'm not taking that medication that gives you a boner for a thousand hours. Have you ever seen the side effects?' And I said no, I had not seen the side effects, and he said, 'Well, believe me. There are a lot of side effects. Dangerous ones.' That man gets nervous taking Tylenol, so I know he won't come around to trying any medication. One time I got very emotional and I said, 'Well, I'm just going to find a lover, then!' As if I could. But I said it like I really meant it and Don said, 'I understand why you would say that, but I hope you don't, Rosemary. I do love you.'"

She sighs. "To be honest, I don't blame him. Every time I look at myself naked in the mirror, I just can't believe it. I am *ugly*! Not all of me, but a lot of me. Lord! Isn't it funny, how we hold these images in our mind, how we think we look a certain way despite all the evidence to the contrary? The other day, I was walking past a shop window, and I saw myself and literally gasped. Literally! Like, I went"—and here she inhales sharply—"and I had my hand over my chest like I'd seen a ghost. I guess I had seen a ghost, only it was the ghost of me."

"You actually look pretty darned good for a woman your age," Dodie says.

"Well, thank you, but that's just it. A woman my age. Sometimes I take out the scrapbook and look at pictures of myself, of how I used to be, and I just feel so bad. I know I'm lucky. I do realize all I have. I believe I should accept things about aging, but when I have those moments of . . . you know, *missing* myself, I'm not thinking that it's natural and that it happens to everyone and it's no big deal, really. I'm thinking, 'What did I do to deserve *this*?'

"Then, to add to it, I feel bad about myself for feeling bad about myself. It makes me remember when I was in the hospital for my cholecystectomy and I was next door to a woman who had cancer. And it was a bad diagnosis, she was going to die, all her relatives would come out of her room crying after they'd visited with her. She was really suffering. I could hear her crying out sometimes. And there I was, a woman who'd had a common and really very simple operation, pressing my call bell for pain medication the moment it was due. I felt so guilty, and I told that to my nurse. She was the nicest nurse, a young girl, really, but a wise soul. She said, 'You know what? That woman's pain being greater than yours doesn't make your pain any less. She deserves the best we can offer, and so do you. Now roll over and hike up your johnnie.'

"What she said helped me then. But this is a separate issue. Now it's shame about something I can't do anything about. I work so hard to make myself look good. But my husband stares at me sometimes, and I can just about hear him thinking, 'Lord, she's gone downhill. I married a beautiful woman and look what's happened.' Things have gone downhill for him, too, but you know how it is. Men don't care. And women are gracious enough not to care, either, at least not about them getting older. But us! What happens to us! I'm afraid to turn my back to him because he'll see how saggy and square my butt has gotten. I won't wear shorts because he'll see my spider veins. I turn out the lights when I come to bed lest I lean over him for something and he sees my face look like it's melting right off. And those damn whiskers on my chin!"

"I have these kind of wart-y things under my arms," Gretchen says.

"Like, flesh-colored things, just hanging there?" Joanie asks.

"Exactly. Do you have them?"

"No," Joanie says, "but I've seen them. Skin tags."

"Oh, great, that makes me feel a lot better," says Gretchen, "that you've *seen* them."

"All of us over a certain age have things we'd rather not display," Rosemary says. "And as much as I sometimes feel like I've reached critical mass, I know it *is* going to get worse. But in spite of that, I just feel like it's too soon to not have any sexual pleasure in my life.

"So last week I gave myself a good talking-to. I said to myself, 'Rosemary, there is more to sex than bodies. Just get in there and try! Maybe he just needs a little jump start.'

"I made us a real good surf-and-turf dinner just like you

get at over at Teddy's. I even made a relish tray with cream-cheese-celery and olives and pickled beets like they do, and I put three different salad dressings in the carousel with little ladles—"

"Where'd you get the carousel?" Dodie asked.

"At Teddy's. They sold me one."

"Really!" said Dodie. "I've been looking for one of those for years."

"*Anyway*," Rosemary says, "I made us a good dinner, and I poured us a lot of wine. At bedtime, I went in the bathroom and put on this black nightie I'd hauled out that I've had for forty years—it's the sexiest thing. It ties over the boobs, okay? A little bow tie. All the guy has to do is pull on the string and there they are. Used to be Don loved that gown. I hadn't worn it in over twenty years and I found that my boobs had moved quite a bit lower from the last time I'd had it on. Bill Clinton was president the last time I wore it. Still, I put it on, and I put on red lipstick and mascara and foundation and blush and I came out of the bathroom swinging my hips, okay? I was swinging my hips like Marilyn Monroe. I'd pretty much talked myself into something, I was feeling confident. And very excited. And very drunk.

"Well, I came into the bedroom and he was lying in bed, fiddling with his phone—honestly, those phones have become adult pacifiers. But anyway, he's looking at his phone. And there I am in all my glory, I even had perfume on. Did I mention that? On my *thighs*. So I stood there a while and then I said, 'Hey, Tarzan! Jane's here. How about we do some swinging?'"

The room is very still and then Rosemary says, "I know. You can laugh."

There are a few snickers, but Gretchen says, "Well, I think that was very fun and creative."

"Yeah," Rosemary says. "He thought it was pretty fun, too, pretty fun*ny*. I could tell he wanted to laugh. But to his credit, he said, 'Well, look at *you*.' And I shook my body all around and . . . you know, did some things like I was a stripper. And under the covers I could see it start to rise.

"I thought, 'Hallelujah!' and I lay down on the bed and I told him to turn out the light and he said why and I said just turn out the light and then we tried, but in the end he was like a floppy fish and I think it humiliated him to high heaven. You can just imagine how I felt when I went back into the bathroom to put my flannel nightie on. I went to take my makeup off and my lipstick was smeared all over my face. I looked ridiculous. I felt ridiculous. When I came out, he was asleep. Or pretending to be. And I thought, Well, that's that.

"But here's the problem. I am still just beset by these urges. I feel this rising up, like a wave of . . . of . . ."

"Horniness?" Toots says, licking off her fork in a manner that could be called lascivious.

Rosemary glares at her. "Yes, Toots. It's horniness. And I don't know what to do about it."

"Well, that's easy," says Karen. "Get a 'massager.' You can get it on Amazon. My friend in St. Louis got one from them that looks like an ice cream cone and she said it works *really* well. Really saves time. And it is *not* a sin. She told me she allows herself to use it in between loads of laundry so she'll be happy about doing the laundry."

"That very notion just makes me feel sick," Rosemary says.

"Oh, for God's sake," says Dodie. "Everybody mas-tur—"

"Don't say that word!" Rosemary says. "Oh, I hate that word. I don't want to hear that word! It's like someone sticking out their fat tongue and speaking around it and drool is all coming down!"

Dodie sighs. "Fine. Everybody self-pleasures, people and animals, too."

"Not everyone," Rosemary says.

"Who doesn't?" asks Toots.

Silence, and then, "Fish," says Rosemary.

"Are you sure?" asks Maddy. "I'm going to google it." She pulls her phone from her purse and everyone starts talking.

"Dolphins!" Maddy yells. "They do it!"

Toots bangs her hand on the table. "Order! Order! Maddy, put away your phone. We're supposed to have our phones turned off at Club!"

Iris raises her hand. "Rosemary?"

"What." Her voice is miserable.

"I just want to say that I think you did a good and noble thing. I do! And maybe the only thing is . . . May I offer a post-game analysis?"

"Might as well," Rosemary says. "Everybody else is saying everything else."

"I think . . . well, maybe you should have let him leave the lights on. I think he was seeing you in a way that you weren't seeing yourself. And I think that for a woman to project confidence about her body is the sexiest thing she can do."

Dodie says, "That's exactly it! I was just sitting here trying to remember this movie where there's this beautiful young woman standing sideways in front of a full-length mirror looking at herself naked. I think she's Italian or something, she has an accent. But anyway, she's just had sex and her lover is still lying in bed and she says to him that she really wishes she had a potbelly. That's the kind of attitude you need!"

"Oh, don't worry, I have a potbelly, all right," Rosemary says. "I have a *cauldron* belly. I just hide it well."

"So maybe you should feel that your belly is sexy, no matter how it looks," Dodie says.

"Well, it's not *sexy*," Rosemary says. "For Pete's sake."

"Then just pretend!" says Dodie. "Far as I can see, ninety-nine-point-nine percent of sex is pretend."

Rosemary turns to Dodie. "Do you still have sex?"

"Oh, good grief, no. No!"

"Do you miss it?" Rosemary asks.

Dodie folds her hands on the table. "You know what I miss?"

"What?" Rosemary asks, in a near whisper.

"Ice cream. That's what I miss. I'll tell you what, I can't wait to get a terminal illness where I need to gain weight so I can eat all the turtle sundaes I want. I hope I'll still want them then. But to answer your question, no. I don't miss sex. I miss companionship. I miss being able to sit in a room with someone for hours and not have to say a word, but feel that someone's right there who knows me real good. And me him. That's what I miss."

"We know you real good, Dodie," says Toots.

"I know you do, but it's not the same," Dodie says. "But, oh, girls, I hope you know how much I appreciate each and every one of you."

A long silence, and then Rosemary sighs and says, "I'm going to have more dessert. Anyone else?"

"Yes!" they all say.

"All rise," says Rosemary. And then, "Hey, get it?"

What Happens Here Doesn't Necessarily Stay Here

John made it to Las Vegas in good time, but he can't seem to get farther. No one will pick him up. He has spent all day at the side of the road—no luck, with even the truckers passing him by. Maybe he's gotten too dirty, despite his efforts to keep clean.

If he could find some work, he could get enough money to help. He could get a new shirt, maybe a new pair of jeans. He doubts he'd get enough for a motel room. It's been easier to get day jobs in other cities. Here, in the city where people make a religion of luck, he's had none.

He sits on a bus stop bench to count what money he has—a little stash he was handed by a sympathetic drunk coming out of a casino. Thirty-seven dollars. Enough for a few meals, anyway. He'll eat after he rests for a while, then find a place to sleep. He knows there are shelters for the homeless here, but he won't use them any more than he did anywhere else he's lived. Too much happens there: Theft. Sexual advances. The prospect of lying next to someone who snores or talks all night. Fights. No, he'll find somewhere outside. He has a blanket, a warm woolen one he found for three dollars. Same place he found a book of poems by Ted Kooser. It was a thin volume, and a paperback, easy to carry, so he bought it. Fifty cents for your soul to take a trip to the stars.

He leans his head back and closes his eyes, then opens them when he hears someone settling in beside him. He looks over to see an older woman, maybe in her seventies. She has jet-black hair and eyebrows, an emphatic *no* to gray. A lot of makeup. A lot of perfume. Black pants, a white shirt, a red bow tie; he guesses she works in one of the casinos. She's holding a bag of food and the smells remind John of how hungry he is. His stomach growls and he puts his hand over it. "Excuse me," he says.

She laughs and looks over at him. Gorgeous eyes, a clear green. "Don't apologize—that doesn't bother me!"

He smiles at her and she cocks her head, taking him in. "Are you hungry?" she asks.

He shrugs.

"Here," she says, holding out the bag. "It's prime rib. The chef gives it to me all the time, and to tell the truth I'm tired of it." She puts the bag on his lap. "Got some twice-baked potato in there, and some creamed spinach, too. It's good!"

"Wow," he says. "Thank you."

They sit in silence for a while, and then the woman says, "You handy at all?"

"A bit. Do you need something done?"

The woman ticks things off on her fingers. "Regrout the showers. Paint the white trim in the hallway. Fix a little nick in the kitchen wall. Can you do that?"

"I can."

"Well, then come with me. You might as well have a shower and wash your clothes, too."

He hesitates, and she says, "I'm not looking for anything else, and I trust you aren't, either. Are we clear?"

"We're clear."

"I'll give you breakfast in the morning, and then you're out. Okay?"

"Okay."

"I'm Trudy. What's your name?"

"John. John Loney."

The bus appears, and she stands. "Don't sit with me. I like to put my feet up on the seat if I can. Just get off the bus when I do. And I'll pay your bus fare—I got a card."

John settles himself in the seat across from Trudy. He doesn't know why he gets these lucky breaks all the time. But he'll take them.

He looks out the window until they arrive at the quiet street where the woman's condo is. It's a clean white building, maybe twenty stories, nicely landscaped; he's pretty sure there's a pool in the back. They get into the elevator together and the woman pushes the button for the top floor. "Life of Riley, huh?" she says. And then, "I like to help folks out. I'm just an old hippie, you know? And anyway, doing good always does seem to come back to me. You know. Karma."

"Right," he says.

She opens the door to the condo. "Straight down the hall, last room on the left is the guest bathroom. Take yourself a good shower. There's a bathrobe on the hook in there. Probably be a bit small for you but it'll do until we get your clothes clean. I got a little guest room opposite the bathroom. You can sleep in there. I'll give you a toolbox and the paint supplies you'll need. Now, I'm going to lock my bedroom door tonight. I'm a real good judge of character, but I'm going to lock my bedroom door."

"I don't blame you. Though you might do better to lock me in rather than yourself."

She thinks about this then says, "Aw, hell, you won't do me wrong, will you?"

"I won't. I'll clean up and then I'll get going on what you need done. Let me know if you think of anything else."

"All right. But before you start, eat your dinner. I'm going to heat it up and put it on a plate for you. It'll be ready by the time you're out of the shower. Then my charity work is over and I'm going to watch HGTV. It makes me hopeful to watch that channel. I like *Fixer Upper* and *Home Town*. Lord. We need to fix and to *value* things."

When John comes out of the shower, Trudy has just finished setting a place for him at the table. Seeing him come into the kitchen, she gestures for him to sit down.

"Perfect timing," she says. She loads a plate up and puts it before him. Prime rib and all the fixings, the gold-rimmed plate on a pink scalloped placemat.

He sits, cuts into the meat, and looks at her expectantly. She's taken the seat opposite him. He'd thought she'd go into her bedroom—everything he needs for his work is on the kitchen counter. But she sits opposite him and watches him eat.

"I feel bad eating all this in front of you," he says. "And you with nothing."

"Me with nothing, huh?" She laughs, a smoker's laugh, and goes to a cupboard. She pulls out a bottle of Jack Daniel's and pours herself a few fingers' worth, then sits down again.

"Better?" she asks.

He gestures to his plate. "I'll gladly share."

"No need." She takes a drink, leans back in her chair, and sighs.

"You're an awfully handsome man—anyone ever tell you that?"

"Some people have."

"What do you think of that?"

"What do I think of it?"

"Yeah, what do you think when people tell you that?"

"I dunno—I guess I don't think of it at all. It's nothing I admire about myself. A trick of genes is all it is."

"Well, you're a good-looking man."

"Thank you."

"I had me a good-looking man once. He and I got together later in life, but he got sick. Lung cancer. I took care of him the best I could but I lost him, and then I couldn't be in Texas anymore. I came here and got a job ferrying drinks, and now I'm just waiting for my time to come. I'm not too sad—I feel like I got a good ride out of life, but everything that meant the most to me is over now. I got my job over there with all the knuckleheads, I watch my shows. Sometimes I babysit for the young couple down the hall—they have a couple of three-year-old twins; they're an awful lot of fun. But I know I'm circling the drain."

John starts to say something and she holds up a hand. "It's true. I don't mind. Too many people carry on about dying when they've had a good long life, and I can't for the life of me figure out why. What do we expect?"

Silence, then, and John supposes her question is not rhetorical. "I guess we expect that even if we live a life full of disappointment, we'll get what we want in the end."

She shrugs. "Maybe it happens, sometimes. What do you want, John, before you head out to who knows where?"

He focuses on his plate. "I don't think about what I want, really." Dangerous to do that. Dangerous for a man who screws everything up to want something.

She takes a swallow of her drink and then leans in closer to him. "I got a feeling about you. You aren't like most of the others I see. You're alive in there. You ought to think about what you want, and then go and get it while there's still time. You deserve it."

He looks up at her, surprised.

"Like I told you, I'm a good judge of character."

"I'm not much of a good sort," he tells her.

"Sure you are. Look at the way you hold your knife and fork. You got manners. You're sensitive. You speak real nice. Someone raised you right." She takes one last swallow, then gets up to put her glass in the dishwasher. "Rinse your dishes and put them in here when you're done," she says. "Your clothes are in the dryer; it'll buzz when they're done. Clean out the lint trap. And don't forget to prep well before you paint. Last time someone painted for me, she didn't prep and it was a messy job. Plus she stole my favorite lipstick."

"That's a shame," John says, and he means it most sincerely.

"Aw, it was just a lipstick," she says. And then, yawning, "Good night."

"Good night." After she leaves, he sits still for a moment. People surprise him, they still do. The good side of them and the bad side of them. He eats a bite of potato, more meat, spinach.

By God, it's good!

In the morning, Trudy knocks at his door, awakening him. He hasn't slept so soundly in he doesn't know how long. He washes up, shaves, dresses in his clean clothes, strips the bed, folds the sheets neatly, and carries them into the hall. "Would you like me to put these in the washer?" he asks. Trudy is busy at the stove scrambling eggs. He's not hungry, since he ate so much last night. He's not used to eating this much. But he'll eat those eggs.

Trudy's dressed in jeans and a flowered blouse, no makeup. He wants to tell her she looks lovely that way, but better not.

"Just leave the sheets in the bedroom," she tells him. "I'll get to them later. You've earned some breakfast; you did a real nice job."

She eats breakfast with him, and she piles jam high on her toast like his mother used to do. In honor of them both, he does the same thing.

"I've got to make a run to Walmart," she says. "I'll give you a ride out to the highway, if you want. You're hitching, right?"

"Right."

"I figured you weren't staying here."

"No. Headed for San Francisco."

"Well, I'll take you to the highway."

It's cool on the highway this early in the morning. John is glad for his fatigues jacket. He's been standing there for just a few minutes when he sees someone across the road push a dog out of their car, then speed off. The dog is a skinny black mutt, fairly good size, and it's confused. It starts to run after the car, then stops. A semi rushes by and the dog crouches down low, shaking. It will get killed out here.

John crosses the road, holds out his hand, and speaks gently, calling the dog to him. After a moment, the dog begins to come, half crawling. Poor creature. When the animal is close enough, John can see she's a female, all ribs and hopeful eyes. Poor creature.

Well, she's his now. He makes a collar and leash from his belt. Then he stands at the side of the road and sticks out his thumb again. The first truck to come pulls over.

"Okay if the dog comes along?" John asks.

"Yeah, sure, the dog is why I stopped," the driver says. After John lifts the dog in, the driver takes a better look. "That dog's starving."

"I know," John says. "I just saw someone dump her from a car, and I worried she'd get hit."

"We ought to feed her," the man says. "I'm Grundy, by the way."

"John. And I agree we ought to feed her."

"There's a rest stop coming up has a pretty nice grocery section," Grundy says. "We'll fix her up. Tell you what, I'd like to get my hands on people who do that to a dog. She's lucky you were there—she would have been hit for sure. Fact, you ought to name her Lucky."

"I was thinking of 'Karma,'" John says.

"That's good, too."

John puts his hand under the dog's muzzle. "What do you say, is it Karma, then?" The dog wags her tail, just a short little movement, one time. John pats his lap and she hesitates, then lies down, her muzzle on his knee, but looking anxiously up at him. He supposes she's ready for reproach. But "Good girl," he tells her, and strokes her head.

"Nice dog," Grundy says. "She's got retriever in her."

"I thought so, too," John says. "Flat coat."

"That stop I told you about is twenty miles away. They got canned food or dry. I think we should give her the canned food right away, and we'll take some dry to carry along. You got any money?"

"I do, a bit over thirty dollars."

"We'll get her a harness and a leash, too. I don't like collars pulling on a dog's neck the way they do. There are some nice harnesses you can buy. If you ain't got enough, I'll kick in." Grundy looks over at the dog. "Ain't that right, Karma? You're all right now." He looks over at John. "Where you headed?"

It only occurs to John now that they're going in the opposite direction of where he was headed. But he says, "This way, I guess."

The men fall into silence, the dog sleeps, and John thinks about Trudy, resigned to her life ending in Las Vegas, her great love lost. And him? What about him?

He closes his eyes, recalling a time his mother talked to

him about love. He couldn't have been more than ten. They were sitting at the kitchen table folding towels, and he'd just told her about his first crush, Madeline Woodward. He told his mother how pretty she was, with her long braids and her big brown eyes, and how she said she'd marry him and they would have five children. But when he lay in his bed and thought of her at night, it made him sad. Why did it make him sad?

His mother said, "Oh, it's miserable to love, Johnny, I'm sorry to tell you so. Miserable for me, anyway, because I feel it too hard. I feel everything too hard. And what happens then? What do you think? You go from the lovely direct to the pain—you can't help it.

"I hurt when I see the lightning bugs flitting about like a magic show. I hurt when the congregation sings at Christmastime, amid all the candles and the greenery and the incense and the hope of the old story. And och, how I wailed when you were born, Johnny, a beautiful baby boy, just handed to me! A *life*, put in my very hands! I'm done in a hundred times a day, so I am."

She held his face in her hands. "I hope you're not like me. But I fear you are. The Irish, you know, we're a sensitive lot, wrapped in the cloak of melancholy. We're always longing for love, writing the poems and singing the songs, but when we find it, good or bad, it's only miserable."

He smiles, thinking of her. He guesses she was right: things do have a way of getting to him. Everything has a way of getting to him—this dog in his lap, he would weep over her if he were alone, that's the truth. He's a man who feels too much and he's miserable in love, just as his mother feared he would be, and so he tries to avoid it. Still. He crossed the road.

What Babies Can See

❧

Link is at Nola's house, sitting at the kitchen table with her. She's finishing making her card for Tiny and Monica's baby in advance of their finally going over to see him. Iris is going to take them, as Maddy and Matthew left early to go to an art gallery in St. Louis. The baby's name is Anthony Edward, and Nola is drawing flowers to twine around his name, which will be the front of the card. She's already written the message on the inside:

> To Tiny and Monica
>   Congratulations on that you have a new baby boy!
>   May he be smart and funny and a pleasure to be with!
>   We will all help with him whenever you say!

"Can you go a little faster?" Link asks.
"No," says Nola.

Link looks at his watch, then begins tapping his heel.

"You are very impatient," Nola says. "You should take it easy. You see more, that way."

"See more what?"

"See more everything."

She leans back to survey her work. "One more thing," she says. "A bee. He'll like to see a bee."

"He won't see it," Link says. "Newborns can't see very well. Everything is blurry. And they can't see far, either. Also, they like the colors black and red best. Your picture is mostly pastels."

Nola regards him. "You don't always know everything."

"Didn't say I did."

"But you act like it."

He shrugs.

"I think Monica's baby will see the bee. And anyway, she said she would let me hold him."

"That doesn't follow, what you just said. Holding him doesn't have anything to do with what he sees."

"Ha. That's what you think."

"Be right back," Link says.

"Where are you going?"

"I'm going to look on the computer to see if holding babies makes them see better. If there have been any experiments."

"You don't need an experiment for everything. Some things you can't tell by an experiment."

"Such as?"

"I don't have time to tell you now," Nola says. "And don't leave—I'm almost done."

Iris comes into the kitchen, her car keys in hand. "Aren't you ready to go yet?"

"Sheesh," Nola says. "The Rush Patrol."

"We have to get going, because after that I've got to get to the farm to help the guys paint the kitchen. I'm getting so close to being able to move in! And when that happens, we're going to have a picnic supper out there—won't that be fun?"

"My mom told me," Nola said. "We're bringing baked beans. That you really bake. In a special pot that looks like it's chubby. There's bacon and maple syrup and catsup in there. And lots of spices. I *think* allspice is one of the spices."

Link sighs.

Nola holds up her drawing. "Don't worry—I'm done, see?" She holds up her drawing. "I made the bee really big. He'll see it."

When Nola, Iris, and Link arrive at Monica and Tiny's house, the baby is crying loudly and Tiny looks ready to weep, too.

"Whoa," Link says, hanging back. But Iris and Nola rush forward.

"I sent Monica out for a pedicure," Tiny says. "She fed the baby just before she left, but she hadn't been gone more than five minutes when he busted out crying real loud. I changed his diaper. I rocked him. I even sang to him, although that might have made him cry more. I took him for a car ride. But he just won't stop!"

"Here," Iris says, mustering a kind of authority in her voice she doesn't really feel. "Let me take him."

Tiny hands the baby to her and then watches anxiously as she tries to quiet him. She speaks quietly into his ear, then sings to him as she walks about. She jiggles him. She takes him over to the window, then into his bedroom, then out into the hall. Finally, she comes back out into the living room.

"Well," she says. "I think this is good for his lungs, anyway. That's what they say, that crying is good for their lungs."

"I shouldn't have sent her out," Tiny says. "And she *told* me, she said, 'Never mind about me, the first priority is our son. I don't need a pedicure.' But she had such a longing look on her face. And she's been getting up with him even though I tell her I'll get him and bring him to her in bed. Sometimes I don't think she sleeps at all. Not one word of complaint, but I really thought she could use just an hour for herself. Thank God she'll be back soon. She should be back soon. And when she hears him screaming, she'll be mad she left."

"You were trying to do a good thing," Iris says, rather loudly, to speak over the baby's cries. "He'll be all right." She rocks the baby in her arms and asks him doubtfully, "Aren't you tired from all that crying? Want to go to sleep?"

Nola sits on the sofa and pats the space beside her. "Sit here, Iris."

"What?"

Nola points to Iris and pats the sofa again.

Iris settles herself next to Nola, the baby stretched out on her lap. Even red-faced and screaming, he's beautiful. And oh, the size of his fingernails!

"Let me try something," Nola says. She takes out her drawing and holds it over the baby. "See?" she says. "*Bzzzzzzzz! Bzzzzzzzz!*"

The baby abruptly stills, and looks up at the drawing.

"See?" Nola says, looking across the room at Link. "*Bzzzzzz!*" she says.

Link crosses over to look down at the baby. "He doesn't see it, I don't think. He's not really focusing on it. But he likes that sound." He kneels down and makes buzzing sounds of his own. "Good idea, Nola. I'll try it with my mom's baby after it's born. We don't have a control variable or anything like that, but I think the hypothesis tests out. I mean, if it works twice in a row, it's got to be statistically significant."

"Whoa," says Tiny.

"He's going to be a scientist," says Nola.

"*Maybe*," says Link.

The door opens, and Monica walks in. "Oh, *hi*, everybody! How's it going?"

Like a chorus comes the answer: "Great!"

All We Need

❧

Goulash is what Confession Club is having for dinner, and Toots tells the women right off the bat that she used Velveeta for the cheesy topping and if there are any objections to that, let her know. Because if there are any objections, she supposes she could make that person or persons a sandwich. Or something.

Iris clears her throat, but when Toots looks quick and narrow-eyed as a reptile over at her, she says, "Oh, no, that wasn't . . . I actually like Velveeta. It definitely has its place!"

"I agree. And one place is right here in this dish. And in macaroni and cheese. Why people think they need to *quattro* macaroni and cheese, I have no idea. It just ruins it if you try to get so fancy."

When they are having their toffee bars and coffee, Toots looks at her watch and bangs the table with her spoon. "I forget who's going tonight," she says. "Whose turn is it?"

Silence, and finally Toots says, "Well, did we *all* forget?"

"No," Dodie says. "It's me. I'm just trying to think of how to get started."

"Just start at the very beginning," Gretchen sings, in her best Julie Andrews imitation.

"I guess it's more that I need to start at the end," Dodie says. "I want to talk tonight about assisted suicide."

Not a sound. Everyone stops eating and drinking.

Dodie sighs. "I have to talk about this, and I hope you'll let me. I hope you'll try to be objective and keep an open mind.

"Now, I know a lot of people think suicide is wrong. A lot of people think it's a sin. But I don't. I think it can be a reasonable solution to a problem. To a terminal illness that you know isn't going to get better. I don't see any reason to suffer when you don't have to. I believe that when the bad outweighs the good, why, then it's time to move on to the next big adventure. That's how I see death, as the next big adventure. And I'm not just being Pollyanna-ish about it. I think death is natural and even beautiful. What I want to talk about tonight is my plan for my suicide. I'd like all of you who can to help me."

"Dodie!" Rosemary cries out softly.

Dodie holds up a hand. "Now, see? That's what I don't want. Just please hear me out. And then we can all talk about it. I know it might be too much for some of you, but let me tell you what I have in mind. Okay?"

The women all nod.

"Excuse me," Karen says very quietly. "Would it be rude if I got some water?"

"If it was rude, it would be rude to ask the very question," says Gretchen. "Which you just did."

"Get your water—I don't mind," Dodie says.

When Karen returns to the table, Dodie says, "So here's my plan. I want to pick a day and have a party. I really do. I want to have it at my house and I'm going to spend money. I'm going to spend a whole lot on flowers. And a lot on appetizers and a lot on desserts. Because who doesn't like flowers? And who doesn't like appetizers and desserts? I'm going to hire Smackin' Good Caterers—I like them, and they wear the cutest hairnets, with rhinestones on them. They'll do all the cooking and setting out and cleaning up; you all won't have to do any of that. But maybe you could decorate. I want very cheerful decorations.

"I want a lot of good music. Maybe one of you could act as the DJ. I have an old-fashioned stereo, and I have a lot of good big-band records, and that's what I'd like to be played. 'I'll Be Seeing You'—that would be a good song to play. Oh, and any Jo Stafford, and Bing Crosby and Perry Como, too—I always loved Perry Como. And Dinah Shore—she never did get the recognition she deserved for being a very fine singer.

"I want to be at the party for a few hours and then I want to go in my bedroom and lie on lavender-scented sheets and have a one-on-one with each of you. Then what

I'm going to do is take some pills. And here's the very hard part. If they don't work, I'll need one of you to give me an injection. Anyone willing to do that?"

After a long silence, Dodie says, "Well, I'm pretty sure the pills will work. I've done my research. So the other thing is, someone will have to call the funeral home. Will anyone volunteer to do that? Tell them I want one of those pod burials, where you turn into a tree."

"What are you even *talking* about, Dodie?" Rosemary asks. "What do you have?"

Dodie frowns. "What do I *have*?"

"What's the diagnosis?"

"What diagnosis?"

"*Your* diagnosis! The one that you got!"

Dodie blinks. "Oh, I see! No, no, no. Nothing's wrong, other than the usual old-age complaints. No. Guess I should have said that first. I'm just planning ahead. I couldn't sleep the other night and I was thinking about all kinds of things, like how I need to update my will, and then I started wondering how I'll die, and I realized I don't want to be dependent on someone else saying when. *I* want to say when. Oh, I know I could have an accident or whatever, but if it's some kind of serious illness, I want to say when. And how. So I just thought I'd talk about that here, where I can say anything. You're my best friends. My confession tonight is that I might kill myself, but I'll make it as much fun as I can."

Joanie makes a sound that might be crying, but no,

she's laughing, and soon all of them are. And they agree, to a woman, to help if the day comes—if *they're* still here.

Maddy says, "You know what? This is like those extreme tightrope walkers, the ones who go between skyscrapers and mountaintops."

"What do you mean?" Dodie asks.

"Everybody wonders why they do it. I think it's because the relief of their not falling is so exhilarating. And you didn't fall, just now. So to speak. We thought you were falling, but you're not. And the relief is exhilarating."

"Yeah, well, we all fall eventually," Dodie says. "Which was the point of this talk. I appreciate your listening. And agreeing to help. See? Now I can cross that off my list. Now all I have to do is clean out my attic and my basement, throw away all my underwear and the pots and pans I can't get clean anymore, and I'm ready to croak." She points to the platter of cookies. "Pass that over here."

"Can I say something?" Maddy says.

"Of course!" says Toots, who always takes it upon herself to answer any general question.

"I just want to say how grateful I am to this group. The Confession Club. You've taught me the value in opening up, in confessing all the things I used to think I had to keep inside. Including, I guess, my need for other people. I was always so scared to acknowledge that."

"Oh, darlin'," Dodie says. "That's what life is, at its best. A confession club: people admitting to doubts and fears and failures. That's what brings us closer to one another, our imperfections. I remember my first day in high school, three hundred years ago. I sat in a row between two girls. One was real pretty and perfect-seeming, real nice, too. And it seemed like she wanted to be friends. But the one I did become friends with was the one on the other side of me, whose slip was showing and who got just terrible grades. Betty McPherson: she's *still* my friend.

"It's all well and good to congratulate someone on something good that they did, or to acknowledge what's wonderful or exceptional about them. And we should do that; we should never be spiritually stingy. But to say out loud our missteps or inadequacies—to *confess* in an honest way and to be lovingly heard—well, that's the kind of redemption we need on a regular basis."

"You know what else this club does?" Toots says. "It shows that when you ask for help, you're usually asking for it from someone who wants to give it. We forget how ready people are to help. You can talk all you want about the evil spirit of man. But I don't think it's true. I think most of us are just dying to be good. And one way we can do that is to forgive the bad in others as well as in ourselves. I don't say don't hold people accountable. Help them be accountable. But to say those words to yourself or another? 'I forgive you'? Most powerful words in the world."

Maddy is quiet. Then she says, "I'm . . . I think I might cry."

"Good!" says Toots. "First off, crying is good for you; it releases stress hormones. Secondly, I have the prettiest hankies all ironed and stacked up in my dresser drawer. Let me run upstairs and get one."

"Bring down a few," Gretchen says.

The women begin speaking, low-voiced and hesitant at first, then louder and faster. The cookie tray goes round and round.

Outside, the moon rises. The wind is still. All over town, leaves hang on trees like open hands.

Oh, What a Beautiful Morning

❧

All morning, it rained hard; the drops fell like little bullets. The workmen doing the gutter work as well as those painting the outside of the house stayed away. In a fit of charity, Iris told the men who've been working indoors to take the day off, too. Remarkably, as promised, the house is nearly finished after only six weeks.

She's bought furniture and fixtures and appliances, and all the walls are painted in the creamy white color she decided upon. She's bought new towels and linens, more pots and pans and cooking utensils. She picked out a pleasing mismatch of dishes from various thrift stores. "They speak the same language," Maddy said, about the dishes. "But they're not all saying the same thing." Leave it to Maddy to understand such things. She is as irrationally nuts about bowls as Iris is, especially ones with polka dots. She even photographed a stack of bowls and framed it for Iris.

The only thing Iris hasn't decided upon is a bed. She

has said it's confusing trying to figure out which kind to get. But the truth is that she likes sleeping downstairs, in John's old bed. She likes the scent of the hay. She likes the memories, though they hurt a bit, too.

Today Monica and Tiny and their baby are coming for lunch. It had looked like they'd need to eat inside, but then, about fifteen minutes before they were due, the sun came out. So now Iris, wearing her gardening clogs and one of Lucille Howard's gingham aprons over her jeans and T-shirt, is setting the picnic table she bought for the backyard. She figures the inconvenience of a little mud pales next to the sight of acres of land and a true-blue sky, a color Nola calls *wowsome*. Out here, they'll see the curious llamas lined up along the fence line and the chickens gossiping in their noisy cliques. They'll see waving wildflowers, they'll enjoy the scent of the wet earth, and they'll have the opportunity to view close-up the air and water show put on by the birds and the bees and the butterflies — Iris likes nothing more than to watch birds bathe in a mud puddle. Next week, the baby goats will arrive.

She lays down a vintage tablecloth, plates, glasses, and silverware. In the center of the table, she puts out a big vase filled with things she gathered yesterday: coneflowers and wild petunias and blue-eyed prairie grass. Then, hands on hips, she stands back to survey the table, the land, the house. She believes that what she has created here is an expression of faith in the widest sense of the word. She understands to the bone the value of this particular kind of resuscitation. What a feeling, to have taken a risk that so many others might have advised against, and to have things come out this way!

When her guests arrive, Iris exclaims over baby Anthony for so long that Monica finally says, "Oh, for Pete's sake! Take him! Tiny and I will bring out the food!"

They eat summer corn chowder, turkey burger sliders, and homemade potato chips; and the baby, seated in his car seat between Tiny and Iris on one side of the bench, sleeps the whole time. But then, just as Iris is ready to bring out the triple-berry shortcake, Monica rises up so suddenly from her seat opposite them that Iris thinks she has been stung by a bee.

"Monica?" Iris says, alarmed.

"I'm fine. I'm fine. We just have to go." She nods at Tiny. "We have to go now. Take the baby and put him in the car."

"What—"

"We gotta go right *now*, hon," Monica says.

"Are you okay?" Iris asks. "What happened? Did I do something to offend you?"

"Oh, no," Monica says. "We just have to go." She looks pointedly at Tiny.

"All right. I'm just going to use the facilities first."

"Don't do that."

He stares at her, his hands on his hips.

"Tiny," she says. "Please."

Tiny heads off with the baby and Monica says, "Bye, Iris. Call me later."

She runs to the car and Iris stands there, puzzled, but then starts to clear the table. She'll bring the shortcake to Confession Club tomorrow night.

When she is climbing the back porch steps, she sees something. Off in the distance, at the side of the road, there is a lone figure walking toward her, a black dog at his side. She recognizes the man's silver hair, the lean to the left in his walk, the apologetic set to his shoulders. And yes, she has always wanted to have a reason to run to the man she loves, but this time she stands perfectly still and just waits. Funny, it seems like the same thing.

Acknowledgments

When authors publish books, it is customary that they use the acknowledgments page to thank people: editors, agents, reference sources, people in art departments and on sales and publicity teams, readers, loved ones, even pets. But this time, I'd like to thank just one person, Beth Pearson, who is an associate copy chief at Random House. Book after book, I've had the great pleasure to work with her and to profit from her expertise. Beth, this letter is for you. I hope you won't mind copyediting it!

Dear Beth,

You and I both know that there are a lot of people in the world who care about grammar and punctuation—though not enough people, if you ask me. (I don't understand why *everyone* isn't up in arms over the ever-increasing misuse of apostrophes.) In elementary and high school, I loved diagramming sentences. I loved taking tests about proper use of the English language. I loved the sound of *intransitive verb, prepositional phrase, direct object, dependent clause*. I still love learning about grammar: One of my favorite books is Mary Norris's *Between You & Me: Confessions of a Comma Queen*.

For those of us authors who delight in and respect the language, copy editors like you are indispensable for helping us to get it right on the page. You are like the hair and makeup people whom actors visit before they are seen by the public. You are like the net beneath the trapeze artists. Authors are the friend in need to whom you are the friend indeed. And you rarely get the recognition you deserve.

We've worked on a lot of books together, and I was always glad to get your comments and questions, to work with you to find a better way, a clearer way, and, oftentimes, a more amusing way to say things. It was never work; it was fun! Even though we never met, I counted you as one of my friends.

Now that you are retiring from this job you've held for several decades, I want to offer you a million thanks, Beth. And a million good wishes, too, as you begin the next phase of your life. I hope you'll find joy and satisfaction in whatever you choose to do. But mostly I hope you'll find a way to work on my books as a freelancer until I retire, too.

Much love,

Elizabeth

THE
CONFESSION
CLUB

Elizabeth Berg

A BOOK CLUB GUIDE

Questions and Topics for Discussion

1. After reading *The Confession Club*, were you inspired to host or join your own? Who would you invite? What would be your first confession?

2. What did you think was the benefit of having Confession Club? Is there any place in your life — a book club, a monthly dinner party — that serves as a type of Confession Club for you and your friends?

3. With the additions of Iris and Maddy, Confession Club had members in every decade of age from the twenties to the seventies. What is the benefit of having members at so many different life stages? Do you see any downside?

4. Do you have any area of your life in which you associate with people decades younger or decades older than you? What have you learned from these people? What has surprised you?

5. What are your feelings about John? Did they evolve over the course of the book as you learned more about his past? Did John influence your opinion of homeless people or Vietnam vets in general?

6. What do you think former city dwellers like Iris and Maddy appreciate most about a small town like Mason? Do you personally prefer small towns or big cities?

7. Iris and Maddy jumped to a conclusion about Amy's health. Have you ever made an assumption about someone's private life where the reality turned out to be different than you expected?

8. What did you think of Iris's decision to buy John's farmhouse without telling him? Should she have discussed it with him first?

9. Why didn't Maddy want to talk to Matthew about moving back to Mason? Did you understand her thought process?

10. After traveling all the way from Mason to Cleveland to find his ex-wife, Laura, John decides not to knock on her door. Do you think he made the right decision? Why did he decide not to go through with it?

Burgundy Berry Pie Recipe

NOTE FROM LUCILLE HOWARD:

This pie looks like you want pie to look, and tastes like you want pie to taste (not too sweet and not too tart), and it could not be easier to make. Serve on pink or green depression glass plates, and you can top with vanilla ice cream or whipped cream, if you like. If you don't have any depression glass dishware, I feel sorry for you.

> pastry for 2-crust pie (and for heaven's sake, make your own pie crust. If you REALLY can't make your own, use Pillsbury pie crusts from your grocery store.)
> 1 cup sugar
> 3 T. cornstarch
> dash salt
> 2 cups frozen blueberries with no added sugar
> 1 ½ cups whole frozen cranberries

Preheat oven to 425 degrees. Combine blueberries and cranberries in a large bowl. In a separate, smaller bowl, combine sugar, cornstarch and salt. Stir this mixture into the berries and spread it into a pastry-lined pie pan. Adjust top crust; crimp edges and cut vents. Bake 40–50 minutes, until pastry is lightly browned and juices bubble through vents.

ELIZABETH BERG is the author of many bestselling novels, including *Open House* (an Oprah's Book Club selection), *Talk Before Sleep*, and *The Year of Pleasures*, as well as the short story collection *The Day I Ate Whatever I Wanted*. *Durable Goods* and *Joy School* were selected as ALA Best Books of the Year. She adapted *The Pull of the Moon* into a play that enjoyed sold-out performances in Chicago and Indianapolis. Berg's work has been published in thirty-one countries, and three of her novels have been turned into television movies. She is the founder of Writing Matters, a quality reading series dedicated to serving author, audience, and community. She teaches one-day writing workshops and is a popular speaker at venues around the country. Some of her most popular Facebook postings have been collected in *Make Someone Happy*, *Still Happy*, and *Happy to Be Here*. She lives outside Chicago.

elizabeth-berg.net
Facebook.com/bergbooks

ABOUT THE TYPE

This book was set in Electra, a typeface designed for Linotype by W. A. Dwiggins, the renowned type designer (1880–1956). Electra is a fluid typeface, avoiding the contrasts of thick and thin strokes that are prevalent in most modern typefaces.